San Rimini,

"Know this," the witch intoned to the knight Domenico. "Until you can forget your ambition and sacrifice your own desires for the sake of another, you will know neither the true happiness of this world nor the peace of death. You value your life so much you refuse to risk it for another?"

She withdrew her hand from her tunic in a flash of motion and flung a green powder into his face.

"Then life you shall have!" she crowed.

Dear Reader,

We've been busy here at Silhouette Romance cooking up the next batch of tender, emotion-filled romances to add extra sizzle to your day.

First on the menu is Laurey Bright's modern-day Sleeping Beauty story, *With His Kiss* (#1660). Next, Melissa McClone whips up a sensuous, *Survivor*-like tale when total opposites must survive two weeks on an island, in *The Wedding Adventure* (#1661). Then bite into the next juicy SOULMATES series addition, *The Knight's Kiss* (#1663) by Nicole Burnham, about a cursed knight and the modern-day princess who has the power to unlock his hardened heart.

We hope you have room for more, because we have three other treats in store for you. First, popular Silhouette Romance author Susan Meier turns on the heat in *The Nanny Solution* (#1662), the third in her DAYCARE DADS miniseries about single fathers who learn the ABCs of love. Then, in Jill Limber's *Captivating a Cowboy* (#1664), are a city girl and a dyed-in-the-wool cowboy a recipe for disaster…or romance? Finally, Lissa Manley dishes out the laughs with *The Bachelor Chronicles* (#1665), in which a sassy journalist is assigned to get the city's most eligible—and stubborn—bachelor to go on a blind date!

I guarantee these heartwarming stories will keep you satisfied until next month when we serve up our list of great summer reads.

Happy reading!

Mary-Theresa Hussey

Mary-Theresa Hussey
Senior Editor

Please address questions and book requests to:
Silhouette Reader Service
U.S.: 3010 Walden Ave., P.O. Box 1325, Buffalo, NY 14269
Canadian: P.O. Box 609, Fort Erie, Ont. L2A 5X3

The
Knight's Kiss

NICOLE BURNHAM

Soulmates

SILHOUETTE *Romance* ®
Published by Silhouette Books
America's Publisher of Contemporary Romance

For I., who not only makes me laugh,
but who undoubtedly knows her Versace from her Valentino.

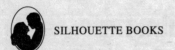 SILHOUETTE BOOKS

ISBN 0-373-19663-6

THE KNIGHT'S KISS

Visit Silhouette at www.eHarlequin.com

Printed in U.S.A.

Books by Nicole Burnham

Silhouette Romance

Going to the Castle #1563
The Prince's Tutor #1640
The Knight's Kiss #1663

*The diTalora Royal Family

NICOLE BURNHAM

is originally from Colorado, but as the daughter of an army dentist grew up traveling the world. She has skied the Swiss Alps, snorkeled in the Grenadines and successfully haggled her way through Cairo's Khan al Khalili marketplace.

After obtaining both a law degree and a master's degree in political science, Nicole settled into what she thought would be a long, secure career as an attorney. That long, secure career only lasted a year—she soon found writing romance a more adventuresome career choice than writing stale legal briefs.

When she's not writing, Nicole enjoys relaxing with her family, tending her rose garden and traveling—the more exotic the locale, the better.

Nicole loves to hear from readers. You can reach her at P.O. Box 229, Hopkinton, MA, 01748-0229, or through her Web site at www.NicoleBurnham.com.

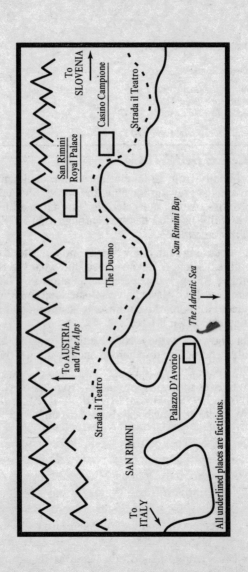

To
SLOVENIA

San Rimini
Royal Palace

Casino Campione

Strada il Teatro

San Rimini Bay

The Duomo

The Adriatic Sea

To AUSTRIA
and *The Alps*

Strada il Teatro

SAN RIMINI

Palazzo D'Avorio

To
ITALY

All underlined places are fictitious.

Prologue

San Rimini, November 1190

Two men he could defeat. Perhaps three, given the element of surprise.

But from his hiding place behind a tangle of low bushes, deep in the richly forested hill country of San Rimini's western borderlands, Domenico of Bollazio counted five men in the glade. Turkish spies, he realized with alarm, noting they wore San Riminian garb yet spoke with heavy accents and carried Turkish short swords. They stood in a circle, kicking angrily at a whisper-thin youth of no more than fifteen years.

A fool's mission, Domenico warned himself, reluctantly drawing his fingers away from the leather-padded grip of his own sheathed sword. Better to ignore his instinct to help the lad and return to his horse. Complete his real mission.

Still, he couldn't help but watch as the youth on

the ground cried out in Italian, begging for mercy. The infidels paid him no heed. They'd come for blood and no doubt they'd have it.

"Where is it?" one of the armed men demanded. His accent made him difficult to understand, but there was no mistaking the threat in his tone. "Make it easier on yourself and tell us now where you have hidden it." He kicked the young man in the ribs for emphasis.

Domenico closed his eyes at the sickening sound of bones breaking. Cursing himself for stopping, for allowing himself to care, he eased back from the edge of the glade, careful not to rustle the thick coat of autumn leaves beneath him.

"I know nothing of this…this message!" The young man's frightened cry carried to Domenico's ears despite the knight's determination to shut out the sound.

"Deny it if you wish. Our spies know the king's messenger was to pass here this morn on his way to Messina."

Domenico stilled, his heart turning to ice in his chest. Still crouched low, he crept back to the glade, his attention once again riveted on the scene unfolding before him.

"Do not let him leave," one of the infidels ordered the rest, keeping to Italian so the youth would understand his words. "If he continues to foolishly insist on his innocence, do with him as you please, then search the area. It's likely in the woods nearby."

Out of habit, Domenico's hand rubbed the pommel of his sword. In his gut, however, he knew any rescue attempt would be futile. The young man rolled on the ground and attempted to gain his feet, but stopped when the tallest of the Turks drove a dagger into his leg.

Anger rose in Domenico's chest, but he had no time to contemplate the innocent youth's injury or his death, which would likely come soon. Afterward, the spies would discover what Domenico had—that the youth's pack pony carried only a half day's provisions. He hadn't the means to convey a message hundreds of miles over difficult terrain.

But if Domenico didn't make his own escape now, the men would certainly find *him,* and perhaps even the message they sought, now safely tucked against his chest, sewn into the lining of his quilted gambeson.

King Bernardo had warned Domenico of the importance of the message, and that there were those who'd give their life to see its contents. Less than two hours after he'd left the San Riminian king's presence, the knight realized the truth of those parting words. He'd be lucky to reach Lionheart and his army, now camped with France's Philip Augustus on the island of Sicily, alive.

Within minutes, Domenico located his horse, hidden amongst the trees a half mile from the glade. He led the animal back to the road, but before he could mount, a noise in the nearby bushes startled him. He spun around just in time to see a panicked woman with fiery red hair crash through the brush.

"Please, my knight," the woman begged, grabbing his arm, "have you seen a young man about? Fourteen years of age, with blond hair?"

The youth. Domenico glanced over his shoulder,

making certain the woman's voice hadn't alerted the soldiers to his presence. When he was certain they were alone, he turned his attention back to her. Judging from her age and the desperate look on her face he suspected she might be the poor lad's mother. Still, that wasn't what set his nerve endings abuzz in warning. There was a familiarity to the woman, though Domenico knew he'd never laid eyes on her in his life.

Keeping his voice low, he asked, "What is your name, madam? How do you come to be near the border? Do you not realize how dangerous—"

"They call me Rufina. Please, I know you have seen my Ignacio. Your eyes tell me so."

Rufina the Witch?

No wonder she seemed familiar. He'd heard of the red-haired conjurer who lived in this area, a woman who'd been fortunate enough to flee the city before being tried for her crimes against the church.

Though he didn't believe in witchcraft himself, Domenico sensed brushing her aside would be a mistake. "I have seen him. Over yon, in the glade. But he is in trouble—"

Not bothering to ask what kind of trouble, the woman turned in the direction Domenico pointed. Before she could take two steps, he grabbed one of her bony elbows. "A group of infidels have captured him. If you enter the glade, they will likely kill you. Wait until they are gone and you will be able to treat the young man's wounds."

Rufina was known to be practiced in the healing arts, though the pious accused her of calling on the

Devil for assistance. With her skills, the youth might have a fighting chance at life.

If he wasn't dead already.

Rufina didn't appear to find the advice helpful, however. She stared at Domenico, her eyes filled with a hate and blame as complete as that of any warrior he'd faced in battle. "My son is bodily injured, yet you did nothing? How dare you wear that sword and call yourself a knight of San Rimini!"

She raised her hand to strike him, but Domenico moved faster, corralling her thin wrist midswing. "I could not. I am on a mission from the king, and to assist your son would have jeopardized it." He swore to himself and dropped her wrist. He shouldn't have even told her that much. "Please understand, madam. Go now, do what's best to help him—"

"Mission for the king," she spat, showing no fear. "You possess a knight's sword, yet you wear no crest of nobility. Is the king's mission so pressing you cannot stop to help someone in need? A young man raised in a humble home, as you were? Or is it your ambition—ambition to gain your own lands and title by currying the king's favor—that prevents you from taking even the slightest risk to help another?"

Domenico started in surprise. In only a few seconds, this woman, this *witch*, summed up his life better than he could himself. And he didn't care for her conclusions.

His horse shuffled beside him, reminding him of his purpose. "I must go now. You would be well advised to—"

"Oh, I shall save him, never you fear. And your guilty conscience. But know this," she shoved her hand deep into her woolen tunic, "until you can forget your ambition and sacrifice your own desires for the sake of another, you will know neither the true happiness of this world nor the peace of death. You value your life so much you refuse to risk it? Then life you shall have!"

She withdrew her hand from her tunic in a flash of motion. Domenico sidestepped, expecting her to brandish a dagger of the type unsavory women often wore for protection, but instead her palm held only a green powder, which she flung in his face. Annoying prickles of fire stung his cheeks as he brushed it away. Probably concocted of poison ivy or some such plant.

Voices rose in anger in the distance, distracting him from the conjurer's efforts to frighten him. This foolish woman would get him killed.

"Secrete yourself, madam!" he hissed, then swung his leg up and over his horse. Turning toward Venice, and the long road to Sicily beyond, Domenico made a fervent wish never to cross paths with Rufina again.

Chapter One

Boston, Today

With any luck, the beauty perched on the brass and leather chair in his lobby just might lead him to Rufina.

Nick Black studied the image on the closed-circuit television behind his desk, watching as San Rimini's Princess Isabella diTalora discreetly checked her Rolex. She kept her back straight and a smile on her face, but he suspected even modern royalty didn't appreciate being kept waiting.

Nick grinned to himself. Her forebear, King Bernardo, wouldn't have exhibited this much patience.

The whine of an ambulance siren echoed up to him, thirty-five floors above Boston's financial district, then faded.

He tossed back two aspirin and chased them with a cool glass of water, then turned to face Anne Jones, his secretary of nearly fifteen years. "I'd prefer not to meet with her personally."

"She's a princess, not some random art collector, sir. She will expect an explanation."

Anne knew him well enough not to add, *besides, you did agree to the appointment.*

And true, he had, in a foolish moment. But if his right-hand man, Roger Farris, could ferret out what the princess was after, all the better. The fewer people Nick dealt with in life—particularly high-profile people like the pampered Princess Isabella—the less his name would be spoken or his picture taken. And that lengthened the amount of time he could stay in any one place, or use any one pseudonym, before people became suspicious of the fact he never seemed to age.

Damned modern technology would get him caught if he wasn't careful, and that would spark an entirely different type of witch-hunt than the one he currently pursued.

He gave Anne a shrug. "Roger can handle it. I suspect Her Highness merely wants to acquire some of my paintings or artifacts for San Rimini's national museum. I've heard she's one of their strongest supporters. If so, Roger knows I expect something in return. Preferably an exchange of pieces. Or manuscripts." Manuscripts that could give him a clue as to what happened to Rufina and help him break his curse.

"Of course, sir. I'll be sure Roger gives her special attention." Anne patted her gray-streaked red hair into place before ducking back into the hallway.

Thank God Anne was so efficient. And she didn't

ask a lot of questions. He'd hate losing her when it came time to switch identities again.

Nick spun his black leather office chair so he once more faced the small television screen. A moment later, he watched as the princess stood and turned toward the elevator. Roger came into view, dressed as always in a well-tailored charcoal-gray suit, his hair neat, his shoes polished to a high shine.

Roger gave a slight bow, then extended his hand. "Princess Isabella. An honor."

The lean brunette accepted his handshake, then flashed him the world-famous smile the paparazzi loved to capture on film. "I'm pleased to meet you, Mr. Black. As you know, I've been trying to schedule a face-to-face meeting for some time."

Her voice glided over Nick like a warm shower after a frigid winter's day. He'd seen pictures of the princess before, but never actually heard her speak. She didn't have a trace of the San Riminian accent he'd expected—her years at Harvard obviously helped her master American English; still, there was a regal quality to her tone, making it obvious she was anything but an average woman.

She was the kind of woman he'd watched men die for.

Her smooth, sexy voice obviously had the same effect on Roger. Even through closed-circuit television, Nick could see the muscles of Roger's jaw working, could sense his assistant's nervousness at meeting the popular princess.

"I'm sorry, Your Highness," Roger finally managed. "But I'm Roger Farris. I handle Mr. Black's art collection—the San Riminian pieces in particular.''

She raised a perfectly plucked eyebrow as Nick guided the camera to zoom in. ''My apologies. I naturally assumed Mr. Black would come to the lobby to greet me himself.''

Roger offered her a half smile in an attempt to hide his anxiety, but said nothing, instead gesturing to the conference room just off the small lobby to indicate that she should lead the way.

Once they passed through the double doors, Nick had only to push a button on his console to switch the view and audio to pick up the conference room.

The princess turned to face Roger when she noticed only two chairs at the black granite conference table. ''He isn't planning to join us, is he?''

Nick couldn't help but laugh aloud. *Good catch, Princess.*

''I'm afraid not. I'm sorry if his secretary gave you that impression. Mr. Black is an exceedingly private man and rarely holds face-to-face meetings. He primarily uses this room to spread out his research materials.'' Roger pulled out one of the chairs. ''Why don't you have a seat? I can get you some bottled water, coffee—''

''No, thank you.'' Ignoring the proffered chair, she strode to the window. Nick could just picture what she saw—her rented Mercedes limousine sitting at the curb down on Federal Street, VIP parking pass in the window, with her driver standing at attention beside the passenger door.

''As I said,'' the combination of her rich voice and stately presence sent a quick wave of lust through

Nick, "I went to considerable effort to schedule a meeting with Mr. Black. A *private* meeting. I flew all the way from San Rimini, leaving my family at a time of great turmoil, and even instructed my bodyguard to remain downstairs as Mr. Black requested, out of respect for his wish to maintain 'privacy in his offices.'" She parroted the phrase Anne used daily to deflect those trying to enter Nick's office—everyone from the UPS man to the *Architectural Digest*-caliber interior decorators hoping to convince the reclusive collector to part with some of his pieces for their showhomes.

Crossing her arms, the princess spun to face Roger. "I realize that you handle his collection, and I thank you for your time, but it's Mr. Black who is the expert on San Rimini's art history. And that is who I wish to see. This is quite important to me."

"I understand, Your Highness, but I can assure you, I have extensive knowledge about—"

"I'm staying at the Copley Plaza. You may contact me there if Mr. Black wishes to see me today." She withdrew an ivory business card from her purse and scribbled a number on the reverse, then placed it on the granite tabletop with a tap of her fingernail for emphasis. "Otherwise, I'll be flying home to San Rimini tomorrow."

She looped her stylish purse more securely over her shoulder, nodded to Roger, then headed for the door.

"Please, Your Highness, it's important to Mr. Black that..." Roger's voice drifted off as it became apparent Princess Isabella wasn't going to change her mind. His gaze flicked to the camera, discreetly mounted in one corner of the conference room. He flashed Nick a look that said, *help me out here.*

Damn.

Before the princess could make her way around the conference table, Nick punched a couple of numbers on his telephone. He watched onscreen as the conference room phone rang. Luckily, the princess paused while Roger snapped up the receiver and listened to his brief instructions.

After switching off the small television, Nick flung open his office door and strode down the short hallway, past Anne's desk and the bathroom, toward the conference room. As Nick approached the double doors, Roger's voice carried into the hall.

"Your Highness, Mr. Black is on his way. He would like to meet with you."

"Thank you," came the silky voice from just inside the door. Then she hesitated. "But you didn't say a word on the telephone. How could he have known—"

"I-I'll let Mr. Black explain."

Roger scuttled out the door, passing Nick in the hallway and giving him a shrug that said, *I tried.*

Nick forced himself not to be perturbed. Roger pocketed a hefty salary to buffer Nick from the outside world. The older gentleman handled his job wonderfully, even going so far as to put his own name on the company's office lease and tax forms. Thanks to Roger, only the very determined knew of Nick's existence.

Determined individuals like Princess Isabella.

After taking a deep breath, Nick entered the conference room, all smiles. "Good afternoon, Your

Highness. I'm Nick Black. It's truly an honor to meet you." He extended his hand, and when she accepted the handshake, he found her skin to be as smooth as her mesmerizing voice.

"I apologize for any inconvenience," he continued, "but since Mr. Farris handles acquisitions and sales of my collection, I assumed you'd prefer to speak with him."

"Glad to meet you at last, Mr. Black. Apology accepted." She cocked her head toward the small camera mounted in the corner of the conference room. "But I don't appreciate being spied upon."

So the princess had a brain to match her beauty.

He flashed her an apologetic look. "I'll admit that I don't, either. Gives me the creeps."

Creeps being the understatement of the millennium. Centuries before, while he was living in a quiet village outside London, England's bloody Queen Mary heard rumors about the man who never aged and sent her spies to investigate. When they reported back that no one in the village knew of Nick's birth, his family or anything else about his background, she ordered him tossed into the Tower of London for as long as it took to discover whether the rumors were true. Only a last-minute escape aboard a ship bound for France saved him from a fate he still shuddered to contemplate.

Though he'd had close calls before, the experience with Queen Mary taught him two valuable lessons. First, that those who discovered his curse would treat him like a criminal, and second, never to stay in one place too long. People noticed. People talked. And he'd be damned if he'd spend the rest of his long, long life being treated like a lab monkey.

He rested his hands on the back of the chair Roger had pulled out for the princess. "As Mr. Farris said, Your Highness, I'm a very private man. Hence the security. Surely you can understand that, as a member of one of the most watched families in Europe? It's my guess that those who enter or exit your palace are under constant surveillance. And by more sophisticated equipment than I possess. I hope you won't consider my methods to be 'spying.'"

"Touché, Mr. Black." She flashed him a quick smile, letting him know he'd broken the ice, then sat in the chair he held out. "Why don't we get down to business?"

He took the other seat. "Please, call me Nick."

She smoothed her dress, a deceptively simple beige silk sheath he suspected cost even more than the string of pearls looped around her neck. "Of course…Nick. Allow me to be blunt. I'm here to invite you to San Rimini."

He fought to keep the surprise from his face. People generally expressed interest in his collection, not him personally, and he liked to keep it that way. Besides, the last place on earth he wanted to visit was San Rimini. He'd suffered too much personal loss on that soil ever to go back, unless something or someone there could break his curse. The impeccably groomed princess before him didn't appear to be in the curse-breaking business.

He folded his hands on the table. "I'm afraid I don't give lectures, if that's what you're looking for."

"Nothing like that. I could have called with such

a request. What I propose should be far more interesting to you."

The princess knew how to bait a hook. "Which is?"

She leaned back in her chair, though her back and shoulders remained in model-perfect alignment. He wondered if she'd spent her entire childhood being coached on proper posture or if it came naturally to her.

"As you know, Nick, the diTalora family has held the throne of San Rimini for nearly a thousand years, ever since the country gained its independence. In that time, we have accumulated a massive private collection of art, artifacts and historical documents. The bulk of the pieces are in storage beneath the royal palace. Haven't been touched in years. Centuries, perhaps."

A shiver scudded along his spine. "Are you looking to sell some pieces?"

"No. I wish to catalogue them. Determine what's important, what's not. In some cases, I need to determine what they even are. Then I want anything of significance to be used for the expansion of the Royal Museum of San Rimini. The museum expansion project was started by my mother, and now that she's gone, it means more than ever to my family to follow it through to completion. I believe you're the man for the job."

Access to the royal collection? Even in his wildest dreams, Nick never thought he'd be offered such an opportunity. He forced himself to remain calm, to keep his hands still on the tabletop, even though his stomach tightened in anticipation.

Princess Isabella didn't seem to notice his excitement, because she continued on with a wave of her hand. "I admit, it was difficult to obtain any of your credentials, aside from the word of some of our university historians. But they have assured me your knowledge is extensive. In some cases, even beyond their own."

So that's how she'd gotten his name. Over the years, Roger had made discreet inquiries to double-check the authenticity of some of Nick's acquisitions. On occasion, when Roger failed to understand the technicalities of his research, Nick followed up himself. Apparently, the professors at the University of San Rimini kept detailed notes about the level of questions he'd posed and about the extent of his private collection.

"So what do you think?" she asked. "Would you care to take on the job? I'd offer excellent compensation for your time, of course."

"I'm certain you would." He rose from the table, his mind working overtime as he slowly paced the length of the conference room. There had to be a catch. A break of this magnitude couldn't just tumble into his lap, not after so many years.

"Why me?" he finally asked. Spinning to face her from the far end of the room, he added, "As you say, you do have a number of experts right there in San Rimini."

"For this project, I prefer to hire someone with a fresh eye. Someone who isn't angling to get a paper published or achieve tenure as a result of working for me. That could color their conclusions."

"Perhaps my conclusions would be colored for other reasons."

She met his gaze, her steady amber eyes filled with the self-confidence royals invariably possessed in abundance. "As a private collector, your best chance to profit would be to undervalue certain pieces, perhaps hoping to obtain them from me for less than market value. But since I don't plan to sell any of them," she leaned forward in her seat, her look clearly meant to let him know she wouldn't waver on the issue, "the point is moot. Also, you're a very private man. I don't envision you using the position to grandstand with the media, or as a means of raising your stature within the art community. If you have an incentive for taking the position aside from the salary or the sheer intellectual stimulation it would offer, I can't imagine what it would be."

Her eyes held a challenge. He wasn't about to answer it.

He certainly couldn't tell her he cared nothing for the artifacts themselves, that he only collected them on the off-chance he might glean knowledge that would lead him to Rufina. If the witch even lived.

Returning to Princess Isabella's end of the table, he leaned one hip against the high windowsill and changed the subject. "Tell me more. What exactly would I be doing day-to-day? And for how long?"

In other words, the nitty-gritty. How many people would see him? Ask questions?

The corner of her mouth quirked up at his interest. "The job will entail systematically inspecting the pieces in the collection, then writing a report for each one. I want to know what it is, its historical value, anything you find important enough to mention. You'll report your findings to the museum's board of directors once a week. They shall then work with me to decide how best to utilize the pieces in our museum expansion.''

''How many people are on the board?''

''Eight. Mostly professors, historians. And the museum curator, of course.''

People who would delve into his credentials. He couldn't exactly answer their inquiries with a casual, ''Hey, I lived it. No need for a degree!''

''As for how long the job will take,'' she folded her hands on the table, steepling her index fingers, ''that depends on you. I can't predict what difficulties you might encounter. Suffice it to say it will be a major undertaking. But you shall have whatever resources you require at your disposal—access to the university libraries, the assistance of other experts— anything you think you'll need. Just let me know and I'll arrange it.''

Nick looked to the ceiling for a moment, gathering his thoughts. The princess presented a tempting offer. But could he risk it? He wouldn't last a week before the board started asking questions. And he had a hunch the princess would soon have questions of her own. Questions he couldn't possibly answer.

Isabella studied him as he began to pace once more, apparently mulling over her offer. There was something dark, something shadowed about Nick Black that sparked her curiosity and, as much as she hated to admit it, her desire. His looks were striking—dark brown eyes that flickered with intelligence, a perfectly sculpted jawline, high cheekbones. He possessed the

smooth olive skin and fine bone structure common in
San Rimini, yet rarely seen in Americans. She wondered, not for the first time since hearing of the enig-
matic collector, if he had a San Riminian heritage.

Despite learning all she could about the man, his
appearance surprised her when he'd entered the conference room. Not his good looks per se—she met
dozens of good-looking men each day in the course
of her royal duties—but his youth. Given the depth
and breadth of his knowledge about San Rimini and
its history, and the rumored size of his collection,
she'd expected a man closer to her father's age. But
Nick's close-cropped black hair didn't show a trace
of gray. If she had to guess, she wouldn't put him a
day over thirty-five. Maybe closer to thirty. Even
though he wore a loose long-sleeved black shirt and
dark gray slacks, she could tell he possessed the lean,
corded muscle of a man in his twenties. It made no
sense. His stature reminded her of a youthful Olympic
boxer or a martial arts expert, but he exuded the aura
of power and confidence obtained only after years of
success and accomplishment.

Even more contradictory, she'd never imagined a
collector of ancient artifacts would sport a giant ab-
stract painting in his lobby or fill his office space with
ultramodern furniture. Not to mention the ultramodern technology. She couldn't help but allow her gaze
to drift to the camera mounted in the corner of the
room. Why did she have the niggling sensation she'd
stumbled into something more complicated than a
simple business arrangement? Like she should leave
the conference room with the same speed Mr.
Farris had?

It's common for executives to have cameras in their conference rooms, she reminded herself, trying to shake off her sense of unease. Nick appeared friendly enough, and he came highly recommended as the world's leading collector of San Riminian art, so it was only natural he took care to document any visits to his office.

Besides, she'd promised her late mother, Queen Aletta, that she'd do everything in her power to revitalize the Royal Museum of San Rimini. If Nick Black could help her fulfill that promise, she could live with being disconcerted in his presence.

"I am sorry, but I cannot accept." He stopped pacing and met her gaze. "Though the offer is flattering and I am truly tempted."

A mixture of disappointment and surprise washed through her. After having nearly every expert in San Rimini lobby her for the position, the man she'd finally selected turned it down. "May I ask why not?"

"The oversight." His voice held no emotion, as if explaining why he might choose a red shirt over a blue one. "If I take this position, it will mean justifying myself to a committee. Thanks, but no thanks. I have no desire to argue each of my conclusions to the satisfaction of a group of men who want nothing more than to prove me wrong. As you pointed out, most professors and historians want to make their own mark."

She drummed her champagne-painted fingernails on the table. No doubt she could find someone else for the job. But her sources told her Nick Black was the best. She'd promised her mother the best.

"There must be *some* oversight," she insisted.

"The museum can't very well display pieces with certain historical claims unless those claims are verified."

"So let me draw my conclusions. When my job is complete, the board can review my work. I'll submit any supporting documentation they might want, but I won't spend my days arguing with them. If they disagree with my findings after they've reviewed everything, fine. They can change what they wish. I won't argue."

She frowned. "You'd willingly allow your conclusions to be changed? Without benefit of argument?"

"I didn't say willingly. No one likes to be contradicted. But if I haven't adequately documented my findings, or if I make an erroneous assumption, then it's their job to correct it. I don't see why I need to be roasted over the coals during weekly meetings."

She pointedly looked at the two chairs. "No, I don't imagine you're the weekly meeting type."

"I'm not the meeting type, period." He grinned, and she found his smile mesmerizing. How could a man like Nick, with such a fantastic smile, lock himself away from human contact?

It had taken weeks of haranguing his secretary to get the appointment, but now that she was here, Isabella found him to be quite personable. And she felt she'd gained the reclusive man's trust, at least a little.

Perhaps she could capitalize on that to make both Nick and the board happy.

"What if you report directly to me?" she asked, brainstorming aloud. "I'll turn your reports over to the board, and if they need to ask questions, I'll relay them. That way, you're available to them as they prepare the new exhibits, but you won't be subject to direct cross-examination.''

"And I'll have privacy as I work? I don't want anyone looking over my shoulder or inspecting my credentials every time I unroll some ancient decree or inspect an old pot.''

"I'll monitor your progress myself.''

When he flashed her a look of doubt, she added, "My degree is in art history. And as you might know, my mother was fascinated with San Rimini's past. She spent a great deal of time at the Royal Museum, and probably knew it as well as the curator. I've always had a fascination with San Rimini's history as a result. If there's anything I'm unsure of, I'll ask questions.''

"You have time to do this?''

She pictured her ink-filled appointment calendar. She hardly had time for sleep, and nearly every meal was eaten during the course of one meeting or another to maximize her waking hours.

But she wouldn't disappoint her family. They were counting on her to honor Queen Aletta's memory. "I'll make the time," she replied. "This museum project is a high priority for me, and I want you on board.''

Nick took in an audible breath. "All right, Your Highness. You've convinced me. But I reserve the right to leave if I feel the conditions are not optimal.''

"In other words, if you aren't given privacy to work.''

Again the devastating grin. He might live a cloistered life, but he knew exactly how to make a woman melt.

"I'll do my best." She extended her hand, and he reached across the conference table to seal the agreement. As his large hand enveloped hers, she noticed his thumb bore a number of small scars. A thicker scar wound its way across the back of his hand toward his wrist. Another mystery to riddle out.

She looked up, and once again found herself captivated by the depths of his coffee-brown eyes.

She broke the contact, then withdrew one of her cards from her purse and handed it to him. "If you can be ready tomorrow, I'll be leaving Logan Airport for San Rimini at 9:00 p.m., sharp. My father gave me use of his plane. You're welcome to fly with me if you'd prefer not to go commercial. Just go to the charter flight desk in the international terminal and show them this card. They'll be expecting you." She hesitated, hoping she hadn't pushed too hard. "Of course, if you can't start right away, I understand."

She could see from his expression that the idea of taking a private jet appealed to him. Good. She'd use the time to further earn his trust. Perhaps even find out a little more about his background before she set him loose in the massive storage rooms beneath the royal palace.

He gestured her out of the conference room. As she passed by him, he said, "I'll be there. 9:00 p.m."

He escorted her to the elevators, and as she stepped inside, she turned to face him one last time. "I believe that once you see the collection, you'll realize that this the opportunity of a lifetime."

"The opportunity of a lifetime, huh?"

He pushed the button to send her to the ground floor, but just as the doors closed, she heard him give a self-deprecating laugh.

Chapter Two

After the princess entered the elevator, headed to her waiting limousine, Nick enjoyed a rush of adrenaline as powerful as any he'd experienced on the battlefield. He couldn't have arranged a more perfect setup! He'd leave Anne in Boston to mind the office, Roger could continue to pore over the historical documents on witchcraft they'd acquired the week before and he'd have all the privacy he ever wanted while he rummaged through the lower levels of San Rimini's royal palace.

He slammed his fist into his hand and went to tell Anne and Roger his plans.

But a short twenty-four hours later, as Nick clanged his way up the metal stairs beside the princess's private plane, he realized he didn't have quite as much control of the situation as he'd imagined. When greeted not only by a uniformed pilot, but also by a bodyguard with the build of an NFL lineman and a well-armed San Riminian soldier, it hit him.

This woman is royalty. The real deal, protected 24-7. Important and very, very high-profile. And she'd just trapped him on her turf.

No matter what assurances the princess herself offered him, his privacy was no longer guaranteed.

The bodyguard strapped his large body into a seat beside the door, while the soldier took Nick's bag, gestured toward the rear of the aircraft, then disappeared into the cockpit with the pilot. Nick ducked through the curtains and past a bathroom, realizing as he entered the sumptuous main cabin that he'd be alone with the princess in the small, curtained-off area.

So much for napping during the flight. A bad fall from his horse he'd suffered two days after meeting Rufina left him with lingering headaches—for which he took megadoses of aspirin—and had broken his nose. He wasn't about to treat the princess to the oh-so-pleasant rumble of his snoring.

Isabella was already seated in one of the cabin's rich leather seats, her seat belt secured, her long legs tucked under the chair with her ankles crossed. A polished mahogany table jutted out from the side of her seat, bearing a hardback copy of Volume One of *The Decline and Fall of the Roman Empire* and an empty crystal water glass.

She wore a simple jet-black pantsuit that made her soft amber-colored eyes and smooth olive skin appear even more luminous than they had in his office the previous day. Her long hair was pulled back into a loose bun, allowing a few chestnut-colored tendrils to slip forward to dance along her cheek. Though it was just past 9:00 p.m. and they had a long flight ahead of them, the princess looked so polished a photographer could pop in any moment for an official portrait and develop a winner.

She cradled a cell phone against her ear, but nodded at Nick as he passed by her to check out the stereo system and small television mounted along the aircraft's rear wall. He hoped to give her a moment to wrap up her call before he took the empty seat across from hers, but the plane's small interior didn't allow much privacy.

From what Nick could overhear on her end of the quiet conversation, she was talking to her older brother, the recently widowed Prince Federico. Isabella sounded concerned about his children—who'd read them their bedtime story while she was gone, how they were dealing with the media invasion on the six-month anniversary of their mother's death—and asked several times how Federico himself was holding up. Whatever the prince said, she didn't seem to buy it, and it was no wonder, given the fact it was only 5:00 a.m. in San Rimini and the prince was awake to talk to her. Her forehead etched in concern, Princess Isabella reassured her brother in a soft, healing tone, then promised to check on her nephews as soon as she arrived. Her love of family echoed in every word. Nick tried to ignore the wave of envy he felt for Federico, having someone in his life who cared enough to check on him.

Once the conversation switched to talk of their father's upcoming state visit to Poland, Nick gave up the illusion of privacy and slid into the leather seat across from the princess. When Isabella hung up the phone and discreetly blotted a tear from her eye, then welcomed him as warmly as if she and her brother had been chatting about nothing more serious than the weather, he realized the publicity the woman generated might be the least of his problems.

How many years had it been since he'd been alone with any woman besides Anne? Never mind a beautiful San Riminian woman with a heart of gold, in a plush jet with a full bar and a nine-hour flight ahead of them.

Nick tore his gaze away from her, turning his focus to the activity in the nearby concourse. Several people inside seemed to have noticed the royal family's insignia painted on the side of the plane and were staring in fascination out the large windows.

"This is the first time I've been to Logan Airport since I graduated from Harvard," the princess commented. "So much has changed. I have to admit, being here makes me a bit emotional. I promise to perk up once we're airborne."

Other than the increase in airport security, the only thing he could remember changing in Boston over the years since she would have graduated was the amount of road construction. He doubted the Big Dig caused that kind of reaction in a woman. Before he could ask what bothered her, she unbuckled her belt and crossed to the aircraft's wet bar, tucked into the wood paneling along the side of the cabin. "May I offer you a drink before takeoff?"

"I don't expect you to serve me, Your Highness. Please, allow me."

He started to rise from his chair, but the princess waved him off. "I'm getting myself a tonic water anyway. No sense in both of us getting up. What would you like?''

"Tonic water's good, but I take mine with gin. Thanks.''

He watched her pour the clear liquid into a crystal glass, amazed that she flew without a flight attendant to serve her, as most of the world's rich and famous did. Princess Isabella diTalora was unlike any royal he'd ever encountered, and he'd known several over his 800-plus years.

She returned with the drinks just as the pilot pushed through the curtains to the main cabin, asking the princess if she was ready to depart. The uniformed gentleman checked to make sure the bar items were locked down and their bags were properly stowed, reminded them to keep their belts fastened, then bowed to the princess and returned to the cockpit.

Isabella took her seat, then grabbed a thick paperback from the pouch on the side of her seat and began reading.

"What, you're not interested in Julius Caesar?" He shot a pointed glance at the tome on the table beside her.

She looked at him over the top of her paperback. "I'm quite interested. I'm *re*reading it, as a matter of fact. But," she raised her paperback to show him the title, *The Future of Independent Film,* "I'm the master of ceremonies of the Venice Film Festival later this summer, and I want to have an understanding of the industry beforehand." She cocked an eyebrow toward the hardback book. "Caesar will have to wait."

He couldn't hold back a laugh. A celebrity host who actually prepared for the event? "Don't you ever read anything for fun? Mystery or romance, perhaps?''

She smiled in return, revealing a row of even white teeth behind her alluringly full lips. ''Who says the Roman Empire isn't fun? Plenty of mystery and romance there.''

''I suppose.'' Clearly the princess had no idea how to kick back and relax, despite being surrounded by luxury. If he was in her position, he'd certainly know how to make the most of it. To his irritation, he found himself wishing he could show her how, though he shouldn't be the least bit concerned about Her Highness's personal affairs. He had a mission to complete and a witch to find. Getting personal with anyone, let alone the untouchable Princess Isabella, had to wait until his curse was broken and he could socialize without fear.

He took a long swallow of his gin and tonic, then leaned back in his chair and closed his eyes. Unbidden, images of the two of them enjoying a night on the town leaped into his mind. He would take her on a picnic instead of hitting one of those fancy restaurants he suspected she frequented with her high-class pals. Maybe serve her barbeque, get a little sauce on her face. Make her wear jeans. Then watch her reaction.

He opened his eyes and finished off the drink, wishing the liquid could wash away his foolish daydreams. He had to break his curse. Had to. How many more years could he go on enduring minimal human contact before he slowly went insane? Ten? fifty? Two hundred and fifty? Times like this, just relaxing in the company of another human being, made him realize just how alone he was in the world. Worse, when he allowed his mind to wander down the path to self-pity, it tempted him to tell his tale, if only so he'd have another person to talk to, despite the likely consequence of being paraded around like a freak, or worse, poked at by scientists, afterward.

"So what do you read?"

The unexpected question threw him. The princess actually cared what he read? Or was she just making small talk?

He straightened in his seat and scrambled for an answer. "A little bit of everything, I suppose." Though lately, his obsession with finding Rufina meant he'd read little more than texts on witchcraft and the few San Riminian scholarly papers he could get his hands on.

"Mystery and romance?" she prodded, a teasing grin on her face.

"Well, mystery."

"But no romance?" She took a sip of her water, then glanced out the window as the aircraft accelerated down the runway. "I hope this isn't too personal a question, but I hope you're aren't being forced to leave a loved one behind while you take this job. If you like, I can arrange—"

He rolled his empty glass in his palm. "Not necessary."

Her tone remained the same, but he could tell from her eyes that she was surprised by his response. "You don't want your family to be with you? Since you'll be in San Rimini for several months, I'd be more than happy to fly them over."

"Thank you for the offer, but again, it's not necessary."

The skin between her eyes folded in concern. "All right. But let me know if you reconsider. I have trouble being away from my family for a few days, let alone a few months. I don't know how you do it."

"I have no family," he finally admitted.

Even all these years later, he still missed them. Watching his parents age and pass away had been one thing, but most devastating had been the loss of his wife, Coletta.

A few years after his encounter with Rufina, when he returned from the Third Crusade, it dawned on Nick that his wife was beginning to age, yet he wasn't. When combined with the fact he'd survived what should have been a fatal fall from his horse, he started to believe Rufina's curse. One evening, after Coletta made a half-serious joke about how she'd gotten her first gray hair before him, despite the fact he was eight years older, he confessed the secret of his longevity. After a long night's discussion, he suggested they move somewhere remote, where no one would question their apparent age difference, which now appeared the opposite of their real age difference.

Coletta was doubtful of his story but agreed, fearful she'd be accused of witchcraft herself should she continue to age while Nick remained young. As they came to accept the realities of his curse, however, Coletta grew cold and distant. She already resented Nick for spending so much time away from San Rimini on errands for the king, and blamed his long absences for her failure to conceive a child while she was young. Ultimately she refused to share Nick's bed. Nick tried to convince her otherwise, before she was too old to bear children at all, but she wasted away before his eyes and eventually succumbed to an early death.

Unfortunately, by the time he pulled himself together, Rufina was long gone from the forest where he'd seen her. No one knew of her whereabouts, or even wanted to speak of the red-haired witch. So he'd spent years trying to sacrifice as Rufina told him he must, working in hospitals, donating his earnings from mercenary work to the poor, even giving up the sword and entering a monastery for a time, in an all-out effort to break the curse. But nothing had worked.

Now, more than eight hundred years later, he still found himself fighting his need for human contact and his need for a family. What he wouldn't give to be in the princess's position. Not to be titled or to enjoy her wealth, as he'd desired during his youth, but for the chance to live out the rest of his life surrounded by people who knew and cared for him, maybe even enjoying the love of a wife and children.

He hung on to the hope that the same modern technology threatening to expose him might also help him find Rufina, assuming she still moved about the world as he did.

"I'm so sorry about your family," the princess apologized, her smooth voice filled with the same tenderness she'd offered Prince Federico. "I didn't realize."

He flashed her a grin meant to reassure, the same look he'd used to dismiss anyone who'd asked about his family over the years. "No need to be sorry," he replied. "I just don't have one. No big deal."

As if sensing she'd stepped into dangerous territory, the princess merely nodded, then returned her attention to her book.

The plane leveled out, and Nick took the opportunity to tilt back his chair and close his eyes. Being caged with the princess for nine hours would make him loose with his tongue and his emotions if he wasn't careful.

Much safer for Her Highness to hear him snore.

Isabella fought back a yawn as the plane slowed to a stop on the main runway at San Rimini's national airport, only four miles from the palace. If she planned carefully, maybe she could squeeze in a nap during the afternoon.

Despite the smooth overnight flight, she hadn't gotten a wink of sleep. Too many problems swirled through her mind to allow for rest, between worrying about her nephews, planning what she'd say to the museum board about her impromptu arrangement with Nick and mentally rehearsing the speech she had planned for the Red Cross benefit at the palace later that evening.

But even if her thoughts hadn't been occupied, as usual, with her work and her family, she wouldn't have slept. How could she, with a devastatingly handsome man snoozing away right in front of her?

Even if he did snore.

The plane gave a small jolt as the pilot cut the engine. Isabella sighed, then tucked her book back into her bag.

"Thanks for allowing me to join you for the flight, Your Highness." Nick blinked the sleep out of his eyes and took a quick look out the window as the ground crew pushed a set of metal boarding stairs toward the door. "Much better than going commercial. Lots of leg room and cushy chairs."

Nick stretched his legs across the space between them as if to emphasize his point, then unbuckled his belt, rose and took both his and the princess's bags from the bodyguard before the burly man went to ready the door for their arrival.

Isabella squinted against the bright Mediterranean sunlight streaming into the cabin and gestured to her leather overnighter. "I can carry my own bag. And you don't need to call me 'Your Highness' all the time. If we're alone, please feel free to call me by my first name. We'll be spending quite a bit of time together over the next few months, and the formality would feel awkward."

"The bag's no problem." Nick shoved her bag higher onto his shoulder to make his point. The soldier indicated that it was clear for them to exit, so Nick waved her toward the stairs.

Fine. She'd let him take the bag. Before taking a step, however, she leveled her most intimidating stare at Nick. "And the 'Your Highness' bit?"

"Lead the way, Princess."

Laughter bubbled out of her, making her feel like a flirty schoolgirl. Clearly the stern look she used on her brothers meant nothing to this man. He'd fire off a shot without a care, unlike most people, who seemed to shy away from witty conversation with her, afraid she might take the slightest jab the wrong way. She admired him for it. Besides, how many times had she asked someone to call her Isabella, only to have them nod and agree, then continue to call her by her formal title? Or worse, introduce her as 'Her Serene Highness, Princess Isabella Violetta Maria diTalora of San Rimini'?

Even the most decorated racehorses had less pretentious names. If Nick refused to call her Isabella, then she could live with simply being called Princess.

As they clattered down the heavy metal stairs, she used one hand to keep the wind from blowing her hair and the other to point out the royal palace, which sat atop a hill in the center of the sprawling town. ''That's where we're headed.''

She turned to Nick once her heels hit the tarmac. ''San Rimini is quite beautiful. Since we're wedged between Italy and the Balkans, we boast some of the world's best beaches, and of course there are the casinos. We flew in over Venice and the northernmost part of the Adriatic just before we landed. It's quite a sight. I thought about waking you but wasn't sure you'd want to be disturbed.''

You were too chicken to wake him, her mind teased. *And you're babbling like an insecure tour guide now.* What in the world was wrong with her? Social situations never fazed her; she could talk to anyone from the president of the United States to the most humble San Riminian nun without discomfort. So why did Nick's mere presence make her act as if she'd had one too many glasses of champagne at a dinner party?

He stopped walking for a heartbeat and stared past her, toward the palace. A vertical crease formed between his eyes, then vanished. ''That's all right. I've been here before.''

''Really?'' she asked once he continued walking,

then immediately felt like an idiot, realizing that as an expert on San Rimini, of course he'd have visited the country. "Have a favorite casino?"

He shook his head. "It's been a while since my last visit. Didn't do much gambling then."

Who visited San Rimini without hitting at least one casino, even if they were in the country on business? "I highly recommend the Casino Campione. They have rooms set aside for private play. I can arrange one, if you wish. My brother Stefano might even join you. He's always looking for someone new to share his blackjack table." She tried not to smile as she thought of the private room her brother, Prince Stefano, favored. It was there he'd met his fiancée, Amanda.

"Perhaps I'll check it out."

Nick took a stutter step so suddenly he was behind her, walking alongside the soldier who accompanied her on all her flights. She looked back, then realized what the problem was before she had to ask.

Cameras.

Funny, she'd never paid attention to the paparazzi who lined up just off the tarmac whenever the royal plane landed. They seemed almost a part of the airport to her. But Nick obviously noticed, and he'd moved so he'd be out of any photographs, his face blocked by the soldier's body.

So much for her suggestion he visit the Casino Campione. The man didn't just shirk publicity, he was downright paranoid about it.

Her limo driver took the bags from Nick, then helped her into the waiting vehicle. Nick strode past her bodyguard and ducked into the other side of the limo, opening the door himself instead of waiting for the driver.

While the driver paused beside his door to discuss logistics with the bodyguard, Isabella turned to Nick. "There are two options for your accommodations. My secretary has a suite set aside for you at the San Rimini Ritz-Carlton. It's only two blocks from the palace and a short walk to the Strada il Teatro, our main thoroughfare, if you'd like to shop or sightsee. Room service is naturally included, but if you'd prefer, there are several restaurants in the hotel or the surrounding area—"

Nick held up a hand. "What's the second option?"

Why wasn't she surprised? She took a deep breath, figuring out how best to explain the accommodations. "After meeting you in person, I suspected you wouldn't be comfortable at the Ritz. The second option was arranged just yesterday, so I'm afraid it isn't quite so lavish."

"I don't think anything is 'quite so lavish' as the Ritz, short of staying at the palace itself," he joked, though there was an undercurrent of tension in his voice as he continued to eye the paparazzi through the limousine's tinted windows.

"You might be surprised."

He stopped studying the paparazzi long enough to give her a quizzical look.

"As I mentioned earlier, the royal family's collection is stored in rooms below the palace. The entrance is in the oldest section of the building, dating back to the late ninth century. It was originally built as a keep to protect the city, but after the Crusades, when politics stabilized, later kings expanded it to create what's now the San Rimini Royal Palace.''

He shot her a cocky grin. ''I'm familiar.''

She felt a blush creep across her cheeks. She'd grown so accustomed to detailing the palace's history to visiting dignitaries, she kept forgetting Nick knew as much or more than she did. ''Anyway, some of the rooms in the former keep were refurbished as guest suites in the 1960s. They aren't exactly posh, but you will have privacy. If you stayed there, you wouldn't have to go through security every day, and you'd have access to the collection whenever you wanted, day or night, without interruption. Now, there are more luxurious areas of the palace, where we usually house guests. I'd be happy to move you there, but—''

''The keep is fine.''

She tilted her head. ''If you're sure. As I said, the rooms in the guest wing of the main palace are better appointed. But they're situated between the family's private apartments and the public areas, so you wouldn't have the same level of privacy.'' She had to offer him one more chance at the usual guest suites, even if she knew in her gut what choice he'd make. It would feel inhospitable not to.

''So long as I have a bed and a shower, I'd prefer the quieter room.''

They pulled out of the airport and away from the cameras, turning onto the road that led toward the royal palace. As they did so, Nick visibly relaxed. She was tempted to say something about the paparazzi, but held her tongue. Instead, she leaned forward and slid open the window separating the driver from the passengers and spoke in quick San Riminian-accented Italian, instructing her driver to proceed directly to the palace, that the stop at the Ritz would no longer be necessary. After sliding the window closed again, she turned back to Nick. "The suites aren't so sparse they lack for plumbing."

"Then I'll be just fine. I'm sure I've dealt with worse." A dimple appeared in his left cheek, and Isabella had to force herself not to stare. Dimples like her father's always appealed to her in a man, and the last thing she wanted was to find any man appealing.

"Besides," he continued, "I certainly can't complain about having round-the-clock access to the collection. If I get an idea in my head in the middle of the night, I like to be able to run with it."

"And that," she replied with a smile, "makes me glad I hired you. But if you do change your mind about the accommodations, let my secretary know and she'll make the switch."

The limo began to wind its way along San Rimini's picturesque cobblestone side streets toward the royal palace, so Isabella pointed out a few of the sights. Nick seemed only superficially interested, so she gave up after showing him the Duomo and a couple of her favorite bookstores and restaurants.

After a few moments of silence, Nick asked, "So, when will I be able to view the collection?"

She sensed he hadn't heard a word she said about the sights. Given his reason for coming to San Rimini, it was just as well. "Today, if you'd like."

"Absolutely."

It'd mean missing out on a nap, but if she got him started today, Isabella figured she'd have more free time to spend with her nephews tomorrow. Besides, the sooner Nick started sorting and cataloguing the collection, the greater the chance she'd have the museum expansion ready to open in time for the country's thousand-year independence celebration, only six months away. Her father would be thrilled to see his beloved wife's dream come true, though Queen Aletta was no longer alive to share in it.

"My secretary will be waiting to show you to your rooms when we arrive at the palace. You'll have a few hours to get settled, have something to eat, or take a nap if you like. I'm afraid I have another engagement and won't be able to show you the storage areas until around four."

He didn't hide his surprise. "You'll be showing me the rooms yourself? I have to admit, Your Highness—"

"Please, Isabella. Or Princess, if you can't manage to call me by my first name."

He held his palms out. "I have to admit, Princess," he emphasized the title, "that I'm still surprised that you came to see me personally, and that you've gone to so much trouble over my housing arrangements. To take even more time out of your schedule is unnecessary."

She reached into her purse, which had fallen over on the limo's plush seat, and double-checked her list of appointments for the day. "You wouldn't have taken the job if I hadn't come personally. I learned that the first time my assistant tried to book an appointment through your secretary."

"True."

"And I did say you'd be reporting to me, instead

of to the museum's board, so it's only natural I should be the one to show you through the storage area. Besides, I'm the only one in the whole palace who can find my way around in there. Most of the crates have been untouched for decades. Centuries, even." She folded the page and slid it back into her purse. "I'll only have about a half hour, but it should be enough to get you situated."

As the palace's wrought-iron gates came into view, she took a deep, contented breath. Nick perked up in the seat, stretching his body so he could get a better look. Though Isabella's royal duties frequently called her away from San Rimini, she never did get used to spending time in hotel rooms. Her own home, where she could sleep in the same room she'd had since childhood, knowing her family surrounded her, meant everything to her.

As the limousine slowed and the driver waved to the guard at the gate, Isabella's thoughts turned to her brother and nephews. Federico had changed in the months since losing his wife. He'd always been quiet and contemplative, at least compared to her other brothers, the ambitious Crown Prince Antony and her fun-loving younger brother, Prince Stefano. But now Federico seemed completely withdrawn and unwilling to discuss his feelings, even with her. His suffering went beyond mourning for his wife, she suspected, and she wondered if her nephews sensed the change in their father. Then again, their own emotions were still raw.

She had no clue what to do about the situation. If anything even could be done.

"Princess?"

"Yes?" She focused once more on Nick. He sat back in his seat and studied her as if he'd read every thought that passed through her mind.

One eyebrow quirked up. "You must be pretty happy to be home. You didn't answer my question."

She plastered a smile onto her face. "I'm sorry. A bit sleepy, I suppose."

"I just asked where we should meet." She must have looked confused, because he added, "If you're too tired from the trip, the storage rooms can wait until tomorrow."

He said all the right things, the polite things, but his hands stilled against the seat cushion, in the same manner he'd pressed his hands on the granite tabletop to still them while they'd discussed employment terms back in his Boston office. And as the limousine pulled alongside the oldest wing of the palace, the section where Nick would be staying, she saw his gaze flick toward the keep's massive stone walls. An emotion—recognition?—passed over his face, then disappeared. Strange, since tourists were never brought to this part of the palace and, to her knowledge, he'd never been a guest here.

This man definitely piqued her curiosity.

"I'll come to your room at 4:00 p.m., sharp."

Chapter Three

Isabella leaned her body against the heavy, arch-shaped oak door leading to the lower level of the San Rimini Royal Palace, wiggled the iron key until she felt it slide into just the right position, then shoved as hard as she could.

"I take it you're going to show me the trick to opening that door." Nick's voice came from behind her as the thick oak started to move.

"The locks were supposed to be upgraded last year," she apologized. "I hate to think how old this one is."

"Original. Door, too. Amazing it's held up this long."

She raised an eyebrow. He spoke as if he'd installed it himself. "You are the expert. Perhaps we shouldn't replace it."

"Depends on what's behind the door. If the collection is valuable enough, and isn't going anywhere for a while, you might consider removing the entire door and hanging it in the empty archway next to my guest room. That way, you can replace the door that's missing there and hang something with a modern alarm here.''

She withdrew the key from the lock and faced him. ''Have you visited this wing of the palace before? How do you know there used to be a door in that archway?''

He gave her an offhand shrug. ''I could tell from the shape of the arch and the scratches along the side where the hinges used to be that a similar door once hung there. Probably so they could close off this hall and keep the drafts down.'' He raised his head and scrutinized the high, wooden support beams and the gently curved stone ceiling. ''Back when this corridor was built, there weren't any hidden heating vents.''

''There still aren't any in the storage area, unfortunately. Prepare to be chilly.''

She flicked on the lights, illuminating a narrow stone staircase leading down half a flight to the lower level of the keep. Nick followed behind her, keeping one hand on the cool gray wall as they descended the aged, concave steps. When they entered the cavernous storage area, she heard Nick inhale sharply.

''I warned you it was chilly.''

When he didn't respond, she turned to see he'd crossed behind her and knelt to study a sword laying atop a blue velvet cloth on the floor, just to the left of the stairs.

''That was returned a few days ago. It's one of the few pieces I've lent out to the museum.''

''That's why it's by the door?''

She nodded. "According to the experts at the University of San Rimini, it's late twelfth century. The museum curator thinks it could have belonged to King Bernardo or to his son, King Rambaldo. I wanted your opinion."

Nick's brown eyes widened in interest. He stilled his hands inches above the weapon. "May I?"

"Of course."

He lifted the sword with care, then ran his fingers along its length. Turning it, he studied the pommel. "This wasn't the king's."

"Which? Bernardo or Rambaldo?"

"Either."

She stepped behind him, leaning over his right shoulder to share his view of the sword's hilt. As she did so, the faint smell of his aftershave blended with the warmth of his skin to launch an all-out assault on her senses. She fought off a momentary wave of unsteadiness, forcing herself not to put a hand on his broad shoulder for support.

The last thing she needed was to feel a man's firm muscle under her palm. She'd made her choices in life, and couldn't allow a fleeting attraction to distract her from her obligations now, no matter how gorgeous the distraction might be.

Purposely ignoring the way his jet-black hair curled behind his ears, she focused on the sword. "How can you draw such a conclusion so quickly? The professors and the curator each had it for weeks."

"You see this area?" Still crouching, he shifted his weight to face her and pointed to the pommel, the round ball at the end of the sword. "Most San Riminian kings had their crest engraved here. Bernardo's was a combination of his and his wife's initials. Rambaldo used a dragon with a crown on its head, though some scholars claim he used a different crest. Either way, a crest would appear on any sword he owned.''

"So who did it belong to?'' She frowned. ''Are the professors at the university even right about the date?''

''Oh, it's twelfth century, no doubt. That's evident from the manner in which it was crafted. Plus, in the late twelfth century, most San Riminian knights had a small cross stamped into the grip when they left for the Third Crusade. They believed having the cross resting in the palm of their hand during battle would give them God's protection.'' He grasped the sword at the top of the hilt with his right hand and pointed with his left to a spot just below his palm.

''See? Here it is. Most knights had the grip wrapped in leather or velvet, so this area, on the grip itself, was protected. Of course, that covering is long gone now and you can see the cross.'' She blinked at a tiny indentation, barely visible on the grip. If she hadn't known to look for it, she'd have thought it to be nothing more than a small ding. But as Nick traced the shape for her with one lean finger, she realized it was, indeed, a cross.

He stood, then offered Isabella a hand to help her up. Once she'd gained her feet, she smiled, intending to thank him for his chivalry, but he took a couple steps away from her.

She stifled a cry of surprise as he swung the sword in front of him in a wide arc. ''It's the right weight and size,'' he commented, as much to himself as to her. ''And the craftsmanship is exquisite.''

He took another step away, then pivoted, slicing through the cold, still air of the storage room with as much power as an ancient knight defending his home against an invading enemy. An exuberant grin spread across his face, again showing off his dimple. "I'm positive it would have belonged to a knight from the Third Crusade. Someone lucky enough to return from the battlefield, given the fact the sword found its way home."

He let the sword drop to his side, but kept his hand firmly on the grip. His eyes glittered. "This is fabulous. What else is down here?"

"Very few weapons, thank goodness. They were taken for the museum's original wing." She hated to think what he'd do with a lance. "The most fascinating items are the documents. Ancient court records, even some birth and death records. Centuries of monastic writings. If you can read ancient San Riminian…" She raised an eyebrow in question, since even most San Riminians had difficulty with the ancient dialect.

"I can."

"Then you'll find a wealth of information that hasn't been studied by anyone at San Rimini University. There are also tapestries, paintings, sculptures… You name it, it's probably down here somewhere. Even old kitchen dishes and palace draperies, though most of those are in tatters." She glanced around the room, astonished as always at the vast collection. "As you can see, it's only loosely organized."

Isabella's mother, Queen Aletta, had ordered the construction of dozens of storage stalls from plywood and wire mesh when she first conceived of the mu-

seum expansion. The oversize stalls lined the walls of
the vast open area. Each had a code posted on its door
that roughly designated the period from which the
artifacts dated, but otherwise, nothing had been inspected or sorted. In the center of the room, all the
artifacts too large to fit in the stalls stood in a jumble.
A few sarcophagus lids and parts of three altars re-
trieved from ancient cathedrals dominated the area.
Oversize paintings, a large iron grille that Isabella
guessed stood at the entrance to the old section of the
palace at one time and hundreds of other items she
couldn't identify filled the rest of the space.

"I'd like to see where the documents are kept. I'll
be looking at those first. With any luck, we'll find an
inventory, or at least a description of some of the
pieces." Nick stared around the room, his face a mixture of wonder and anticipation. "This is every historian's dream. Not nearly as dusty as I expected, either."

"I told you it would be the chance of a lifetime,"
she replied. "And even though it doesn't seem dusty
now, it will be once you start moving things around.
My mother had the open areas of the floor cleaned,
but most of the artifacts were left untouched."

"That's fine." Nick seemed in another world. He
knelt to turn over a small wooden chest, inspected the
bottom, then righted it before moving along to the
next group of items.

"Unfortunately," Isabella explained, "the documents are scattered throughout the room. Anything
with an obvious date was placed in the appropriate
stall, but the rest were placed into crates in the back

of the room. I'll provide you with tools to open them. If you need help—''

''I shouldn't.''

He walked in front of her, boyish happiness in his stride as he peeked through the wire mesh into each of the stalls, occasionally turning to stare at the sarcophagus lids as he went. He kept the ancient sword in his hand, twirling it at his side as if it had been crafted especially for him. Despite the fact he wore a black polo shirt and pressed khakis, she couldn't shake the mental image of him as a medieval warrior. His biceps bunched as he wielded the weapon, and for a brief moment, she could envision him in full armor, sporting a knight's longer hair and brandishing the weapon against San Rimini's enemies.

''Have you always worn your hair so short?'' she asked, then felt her face heat in embarrassment. Her nanny, rest her soul, would roll over in her grave to hear the princess ask such a question. ''I apologize. I don't know what prompted me to ask something so personal.''

''That's not too personal. Asking for my income tax returns or what kind of underwear I wear, now that's personal.''

As soon as the offhanded reply to the princess's apology left Nick's mouth, a sudden wave of panic grabbed his gut. He'd relaxed too much, let his guard down. What if she did seek out his nonexistent tax returns? He stopped walking and turned to face the princess, but intentionally kept his voice aloof. ''I did wear my hair longer once. Long time ago, though. Why?''

He'd been foolish enough to note that the oak door

to the storage room entrance was the original. He'd passed through it dozens of times on his way to this very storage area, which served as the armory in King Bernardo's day. Nick corrected his slip easily enough, but something in the princess's expression now gave him pause.

It was as if she saw him the way he was. *When he wore his hair longer.*

She waved off his question. "No real reason, I guess. Just curiosity. The close-cropped look suits you. It's—it's similar to my brother Antony's, is all." She leaned over to finger a rolled-up tapestry, but as they continued their walk along the row of stall doors, he noticed her discreetly continue to study him and the way he held the sword.

She couldn't possibly know. Not unless she'd seen a painting of him, and he knew for a fact none existed. He'd been a landless knight and fortunate in his access to the royal household. Only the king and other titled members of San Rimini's elite commissioned paintings, not knights merely aspiring to that lofty group.

He inwardly cursed himself for his paranoia and changed the subject. No one in this day and age would believe his story, let alone guess at it merely from watching him hold a sword.

Still…

Holding the weapon aloft, he asked, "Where does this belong?"

"I'll leave it to your discretion. Your job is to sift through this collection, remember?" She shot him a grin, and he realized that even in private, she showed the same clear emotions the press photographers so often captured when she was out in public.

He returned her smile without meeting her gaze, lest he be tempted by what he saw in her too-friendly amber eyes. The intimacy of their quiet surroundings and the memories brought back by the immense collection of artifacts taxed his ability to distance himself from other people, as he'd spent years schooling himself to do. Scanning the room, he spied a desk jimmied into one corner, close to the door. In his fascination with the sword, and with the princess, he missed seeing it when he'd entered. High above the desk a lone window broke the long plane of stone wall, granting it the room's only sunlight. "I'll just put it on the desktop for now."

She reached under the cuff of her white silk blouse to check her watch. "I'll do it. My half hour's nearly up. I hate to leave you alone to forage down here, but I have an appointment I must attend." She reached for the sword, and he gave it to her, half-wondering if doing so was a breach of etiquette. One generally didn't ask a princess to carry a sword.

"The weight of medieval weapons always surprises me," she commented as she took it. "I've lifted this sword before, and I know it's only three pounds or so, but I have no idea how men used to fight with them for such long periods of time. You'd think by the end of a day in battle they'd be as likely to injure themselves as the enemy."

He leaned forward to help her, reaching for the hilt. "Men used to spend years training in order to use them properly. It's as much a matter of technique as it is strength. Here, why don't I take it to the desk?"

She looked up at him, her eyes reflecting the light of the lone window, and he realized he had her hand trapped beneath his.

What had he been thinking? He should have just let her take it to the desk, proper etiquette be damned, instead of touching the untouchable princess. Already his body responded to the feel of her delicate hand under his stronger one, filling with the sharp ache of want.

"Will you show me?"

He blinked, desire sending his mind down the path his body longed to take. Show her *what?*

"You seemed to have the technique down pat, and I've always been curious."

Duh, Nick. She'd spent her life surrounded by displays of ancient swords and armor, living in a thousand-year-old palace, yet never experienced the terror of the real thing as her ancestors had. Of course she'd be curious about how the weapon would be used.

"I suppose."

He swallowed hard and moved behind her, allowing his arm to curl around hers, her back to brush against his chest. The scent of her expensive shampoo floated up to him, and he fought to keep his instant arousal in check. Far too many years had passed since he'd allowed himself the comfort of a woman. The love-'em-and-leave-'em relationships his curse necessitated left him feeling so empty he'd given them up long ago.

But his self-imposed celibacy didn't mean he was immune to beautiful women. Particularly this beautiful woman.

She flexed her hand around the hilt, and her body moved even tighter against his. "Like this?"

"Just like that."

He gave an inward prayer for strength. And not the kind of strength needed to hold the sword.

From the first moment he'd heard the princess's silky voice over his closed-circuit television, he should have been on his guard. If he wasn't careful, he'd be kissing the princess within minutes. And he'd learned enough about women over his long lifetime to realize that she'd probably kiss him right back.

She turned her long neck and met his gaze. Her whisper-soft lips beckoned to him, and suddenly he wondered if she would kiss him first. It occurred to him that a woman like her, living in the public eye and sharing her home with three brothers, her father and a slew of staff and bodyguards, probably didn't get much opportunity for stolen kisses.

He started to pull back. Kissing the princess would jeopardize not only his job, but his peace of mind. But then her exquisite lips parted just enough to ask, "Where do you want me to put my other hand?"

He stared at her for a heartbeat, then the sword clattered to the cold stone floor.

Isabella jumped at the noise, which seemed to echo forever in the cavernous room, and let out a surprised gasp.

"Your Highness! I'm so sorry. Are you all right?"

"Yes, fine." She recovered. "I'm fine. Just startled."

He bent to retrieve the sword. "I must've lost my hold on it. Here," he twisted it in his hand, demonstrating that he had better control of the weapon this time, "let's start over."

The princess backed toward the door, her face several shades paler than usual. "No, that's all right. There are certain things I was probably never meant to learn." She checked her watch again, though only a few minutes had passed since she last checked. "And I don't want to be late to my appointment."

"Well, perhaps later, if you change your mind." So long as she meant learning about the sword.

She nodded, but said nothing. It was only after she left the room he realized she hadn't corrected him when he'd called her "Your Highness."

Isabella gave the guard outside her palace apartments a cursory nod, then disappeared into the sanctuary of her private rooms and made a beeline for the sumptuous Italian marble bathroom, the one room in the palace where she was always guaranteed to be undisturbed. After misting her face with the bottle on the countertop and blotting it with a fluffy cotton towel, she studied herself in the heavy, gilt-edged mirror.

"I must be the world's most famous twenty-eight-year-old virgin," she muttered, then said a quick prayer of thanks that the world had no clue. What had she been thinking, asking Nick Black where she should put her hand? She'd meant on the *sword,* but the instant the words left her mouth, she'd realized the double meaning. And felt his instant reaction against the small of her back just before the sword fell to the floor.

The whole episode rocked her to the core. Yet at

the same time, while her brothers had informed her long ago that men could get aroused without much provocation, and intended that information to serve as a warning, the idea she'd caused such a reaction in Nick thrilled her.

"Stupid, stupid, stupid," she grumbled aloud to the mirror. Hadn't it been drilled into her since childhood that letting her private desires supersede her royal duties only led to trouble? Just look at what had happened to Princess Stefanie. To Diana. To Fergie. If she fell for a man, what would make her immune to the ravages of the press?

And how would that publicity affect her family? The Windsors and Grimaldis still caught flak for their past indiscretions.

Resolving to focus on her duties, she strode back into her bedroom, where one of the maids had thoughtfully unpacked her belongings, taken away her laundry and laid out the silver Valentino gown and diamond necklace she planned to wear to her father's annual Red Cross benefit dinner. Business came first, and for someone in her position, business never ended.

In fact, she only had twenty minutes before she needed to meet her father so they could enter the ballroom together.

She located the notes for her speech, which she'd written on the flight to Boston, read through them a final time, then stuffed them into a small beaded bag designed to match the gown. After carefully stepping into the dress to avoid snagging the delicate beadwork, she slipped the straps over her shoulders and zippered the back. Studying her image in the full-length mirror, she decided she'd pass muster, though she wished she could wear jeans and flip-flops. Not that she owned a pair of either.

A knock sounded at the door, and she strode through her sitting room to answer it, hooking the diamond necklace at her nape as she walked.

"Nerina." She smiled at her secretary. "Come in. I assume my father is waiting."

"Not yet, Your Highness." The older woman gave a slight bow. Though Isabella constantly urged Nerina to relax, the secretary's twelve years in service to Queen Aletta ingrained a certain level of formality into her behavior. "King Eduardo asks that you meet him on the east staircase in ten minutes." After politely inquiring about the princess's trip, Nerina pulled out her electronic organizer. "Before you meet with the king, we should discuss your schedule for tomorrow."

"Please," Isabella said as she stepped into her shoes, then went in search of a hairbrush.

Nerina followed her as far as the bathroom door, keeping a discreet distance as Isabella located the brush and some pins in the vanity drawer.

"At 8:00 a.m. you'll appear at the Catholic elementary school adjacent to the Duomo to talk to the students about the importance of charity work. You should offer some examples of things the children can do to help others."

Isabella listened as she pinned her hair into a loose chignon. "I've already spoken to Father Dario about it. I have several ideas."

Nerina nodded, "Of course, Your Highness. While you're visiting the school, the Greek foreign minister will be holding talks with King Eduardo and Prince Antony. When you return from the school, you're to give him a tour of the rose garden prior to an outdoor lunch. Your father, your brother Antony and his wife, Princess Jennifer, will all be in attendance. There will be several members of the press on hand, so one of your softer suits would be appropriate. At two-thirty, you'll need to break from lunch. Several members of the planning committee for the Venice Film Festival will be here to meet with you to finalize your duties as master of ceremonies. Your father has set aside the palace library for the meeting."

Isabella frowned as she turned from the mirror and grabbed her purse. "Will I have any time for a break? I didn't get to sleep on the flight back from Boston."

Nerina shook her head. "I'm afraid not, Your Highness. Perhaps I can squeeze in some time on Wednesday. It's the best I can do."

Isabella thanked her, but as they strode side-by-side through the royal family's private wing toward the east staircase, Nerina outlined a schedule for the next week so jam-packed Isabella knew she'd have to sacrifice her gym time if she wanted a nap. She tugged at the hip of her beaded gown, deciding it might be better to go to the gym. Otherwise, she'd never fit into her gowns by the time the film festival rolled around.

"What should I tell Mr. Black, Your Highness?"

Isabella stopped walking as the sound of Nick's name popped her out of her thoughts about form-fitting clothes. "I'm sorry, Nerina. What about Mr. Black?"

"I went to the storage area before I came to your

apartments to ensure he had any office supplies or reference materials he might require. The supplies are on order, Your Highness, but apparently you neglected to leave him the chart explaining the layout of the stalls.''

''I have it in my apartments.'' Somewhere.

''I can deliver it to him while you're attending the Red Cross benefit, if you'd like.''

''I have to find it first,'' she admitted. ''I'll get it to him first thing in the morning.'' Which meant another trip to the storage room, and another face-to-face meeting with Nick.

She'd always considered the older section of the palace as an escape, a retreat from the pressures and grandeur of her life as a modern-day princess. A place she could let down her defenses, pretend she was a normal person. As a child, she'd hidden herself away in the old guest quarters to read romance novels without the observant eye of her nanny upon her. As she'd grown, however, she'd spent more time in the storage areas, indulging her curiosity about her country's history without anyone interrupting to make demands of her, as people so often did when she was in her apartments.

But now, with Nick Black residing within the keep's silent stone walls and investigating the recesses of the storage room, her retreat was no longer her own. And letting her defenses down, as she tended to do whenever she retreated to the medieval section of the palace, was no longer an option.

If she did, what would Nick make of it? If she allowed him to get close to her again, as she had this afternoon, would he dare to kiss her?

Because if he did, she knew she'd kiss him back, despite her logical side warning against it.

"You look beautiful, *mi figlia*."

Her father entered the hallway from a side door, his calm voice soothing her frayed nerves, as it always did when he complimented her.

She couldn't help but smile at him. "*Lei è gentile*, Papa. And you look wonderful, as well."

At fifty-five, her father retained the vigor and good looks of his youth, despite having heart surgery nearly two years earlier. His tuxedo emphasized his lean physique, and the dark color suited his flawless olive skin and short salt-and-pepper hair. He extended his arm as they approached the top of the staircase. "And your trip to the United States, Isabella? I understand you found an expert to continue your mother's museum work?"

She nodded, and a vision of Nick twirling the sword in his strong, scarred hand flashed through her mind. "It is my hope he can finish in time to open the wing as part of our upcoming independence celebration."

The king's eyes filled with delight at her words, and he kissed her cheek. "Splendid! Your mother would be so touched. As I am."

As they arrived at the top of the staircase, conversation between father and daughter ceased. The crowd, gathered in the Imperial Ballroom below them, quieted as all eyes turned to the princess and king.

Along with all their expectations.

Isabella descended the stairs on her father's arm, catching the eye of the Red Cross director and flashing him a smile, then nodding to a familiar parliament member. This was her element, the arena in which she shone, and where she could help so many.

The last thing she needed was to spend her evening thinking about the mysterious man she'd just hired.

She greeted one of her father's longtime friends, Count Giovanni Alessandro, and politely listened to him talk about his thirty-something son, as he always did when they were together. She knew the Count hoped for her to take an interest in the young man, but she knew his reputation. How many nights had the Count's son spent passed out in a casino hotel room after gambling all afternoon? He might be the most wonderful man on earth, once he got away from the parties, but she would never risk the controversy such a relationship would cause her family.

She caught her father's eye as he circulated among the guests. He flashed her a quick smile, and she knew he was proud of her and all she'd done.

No, she'd worked too hard and too long to take any missteps now. And while the Count's son presented no temptation, Nick Black most certainly did. As she excused herself and moved farther into the ballroom, she resolved to take the chart down and leave it on the storage room desk tonight, while Nick slept, instead of waiting until morning.

Before seeing Nick again, she needed to get her hormones under control. Under no circumstances would temptation get the better of her.

Chapter Four

Manolo Blahnik shoes dazzled the eye, Princess Isabella decided as she made her way out of the Imperial Ballroom just after 1:00 a.m., but they were never designed to be worn all night—let alone by a teetering woman approaching thirty-six hours without sleep. For at least the fourth or fifth time that evening, she inwardly cursed the fact that San Riminians favored style over comfort, and expected her to do so, as well.

She stopped at the foot of the stairs to pose for one last publicity photo with the Director of the San Riminian Red Cross, beaming for the camera despite the fact her feet ached. If a simple picture of her in the newspaper gained one iota more attention for the organization, she could handle the extra minute's discomfort.

Once safely free of the Director and the palace's public areas she stifled a yawn, then stopped walking and put her hand against a glass display case for support. She stared down the long, oak-paneled hallway leading past her brother Antony's apartments toward her own. Some days, the sheer size of the palace overwhelmed her. She may as well run the Boston Marathon as try to get to her room.

Making certain she was alone, she slipped off her strappy silver heels and hooked them over her wrist. Not wearing the shoes forced her to hike up her long dress to keep from tripping, but at least her feet no longer chafed.

And since her next appointment wasn't until 8:00 a.m., she could finally put her feet up and enjoy a few blissful hours of sleep in her own soft, warm bed.

She smiled to herself as she thought about tucking in her nephews, Prince Federico's four-year-old Arturo and two-year-old Paolo. While the guests enjoyed dinner, and before she needed to give her speech, she'd managed to duck out of the ballroom just long enough to read the boys a new bedtime story, one she'd purchased for them while in the United States. The little princes had been thrilled with her quick visit, but she could tell the death of their mother still weighed heavily on them, particularly on Arturo.

Fortunately, the media had given the boys some latitude since their mother's unexpected death from an undiagnosed aneurysm, but the reporters picked at Federico like starving dogs who'd discovered a meaty chicken bone. Four separate men with notepads at the ready asked her about Federico during the evening's benefit dinner. She'd given them nonspecific answers about Federico still being shocked and saddened, as any husband would be after losing his young wife, but in reality, she sensed there was more to Federico's dark mood than mourning Lucrezia. Too many months had passed to explain his melancholy mood.

She waved to the guard outside her palace apartments, who thankfully didn't notice she wore her shoes over her wrist, then pushed open the thick oak door with a sigh. Federico was a grown man. He'd find a way to cope, and she'd made it clear she'd be there for him once he was ready to talk. The sooner he did, the better it would be for the boys.

And the sooner he'd be able to attend royal functions with her again. Now that Prince Antony was married, he tended to focus on his wife during royal dinners and balls. Prince Stefano had only recently started attending formal events, avoiding them like the plague until his fiancée Amanda encouraged him to take a more active role in palace life. However, like Antony, he tended to focus on the woman by his side.

Still, even when Lucrezia was alive, Federico kept close to Isabella at formal events, not only to keep her company, but also to run interference for her when anyone tried to monopolize her time. He'd have been a lifesaver tonight, when she'd been unable to politely shake a young Italian banker who'd asked her for an unseemly third dance.

Thank goodness the lanky man asked her to dance near the windows, which opened onto the garden. Otherwise, his nervous perspiration might have stained her dress where his palms encircled her waist.

Attempting to push the unpleasant thought from her mind, Isabella set her too-tight designer shoes on the appropriate rack in her antique armoire, resolving to auction them off for charity. Custom-made Manolo Blahniks were less pricey in San Rimini than in the United States, where a pair like these would cost nearly a thousand dollars, but they were still expensive enough and trendy enough to be coveted. And the crowd who frequented palace events could afford it.

She ignored the fancy nightgown her maid left out for her. Instead, she pulled a soft cotton one from her armoire and laid it on the bed, half-wondering if she'd have the strength to change out of her Valentino gown. There'd be no reviewing her notes for the elementary school "how you can help charity" speech tonight; she'd have to refresh her memory about her discussion with Father Dario during the limousine ride to the school. Keeping the banker at arm's length tonight tapped out the last reserves of her energy.

She flopped on her bed next to the nightgown, closing her eyes against the image of her overeager dance partner, but found another image, more powerful and sensuous, leaping unbidden into her sleepy mind.

Nick Black, with his arms encircling her waist, spinning her around the dance floor of the Imperial Ballroom. But unlike the banker, Nick moved with ease, whispering in her ear, caressing her back with his strong hands, seducing her with his mysterious ways. And he certainly didn't leave sweat stains on her dress. In fact, he sent *her* into a nervous sweat as he looked at her with barely contained desire in his eyes, just as he had when he'd had his arms around her, holding the sword that afternoon in the storage room....

Isabella's eyes flew open in alarm. *The storage room!*

She'd promised Nerina she'd have the chart of the stalls to Nick by morning. And given the direction her thoughts wandered, she'd be far better off slipping the chart onto his desk tonight, rather than facing him in the morning. Tearing herself from the inviting softness of the bed, she fished a pair of slippers out of her armoire, then spent a few minutes searching her sitting room for the chart before locating it next to the plush velvet armchair where she'd last studied it. Tucking it under her arm, she stepped out of her apartments into the darkened palace hall.

The smell of dust and aged parchment emanated from the crate as Nick pried the last nail loose, then lifted the planked lid off the crate and rested it against the stone wall. Inside, hundreds of scrolls in varying shades of yellow lay in neat stacks.

"Please, be in here," Nick murmured to the cold room, then knocked on the side of the wooden crate for luck. Somewhere, somehow, there had to be a record of Rufina's life—had she left the country? Had she lived as long as he had? At least he hoped so.

For the past seven hours, he'd pried open crate after crate, his efforts leaving the storage area in a dusty haze. He climbed atop the desk and cracked the window open to let in the fresh air of the gardens, but soon strains of music and laughter floated to his ears.

He knew the palace well enough to guess the

sounds came from the Imperial Ballroom, though that particular room hadn't existed during King Bernardo's time. Even so, the tenor of palace parties remained the same. He couldn't help but imagine the clinking champagne glasses, the intimate conversations and the laughter of couples young and old as they circled around the dance floor under gold- and crystal-laden chandeliers without a care in the world.

He'd met Coletta at such a function, soon after she'd been taken on as a handmaiden to the queen. Though the drink was wine instead of champagne, and they'd shared a lead cup instead of toasting with crystal flutes, the emotion had been the same as what filtered through the palace tonight. The carefree laughter of high-spirited dancers, the whispered promises of young love, and excitement at being invited into the royal circle, which brought with it a sense of belonging. Even after he and Coletta married, she'd continued her service at the palace, spending months at a time at the palace with the queen while he fought abroad for San Rimini, then warming his bed at their village home during the all-too-brief times of peace.

Until the curse. And their break from everything they loved about life, both at the palace and in their small village.

He'd learned long ago to stamp down his need to socialize, but hearing the celebration in the main palace progress while he sorted through ancient scrolls and ledgers weakened his resolve. Thankfully, over the last hour the music had drifted off and the sounds of couples strolling past the window, sharing kisses and sweet nothings as they savored the privacy of the palace gardens, finally ceased. Focusing on the task at hand, he turned to another stack of crates, trying to decide which to open first and which to leave for later, when he'd cleared more space.

He picked up his crowbar, but the sound of the storeroom door scraping along the floor stopped him. He checked his watch, which was still on Boston time, and did a quick calculation. Who could be in the keep at this hour, let alone in the usually locked storeroom? Setting the crowbar on a nearby crate, he strode toward the entrance, skirting the central area with its jumble of artifacts, rolled-up tapestries and antique furniture.

When the door came into view, he froze.

Isabella diTalora stood beside his desk, her lithe body highlighted to perfection by a luminous silver gown. She'd turned on the passageway's light as she'd descended the narrow steps, and with that light now behind her, the wisps of chestnut hair escaping from her elegant upswept style gave the impression of an angel's halo surrounding her head.

The woman looked as if she'd descended straight from heaven. Despite the chill in the room, Nick's blood turned white-hot in his veins. He curled his fingers around the edge of a centuries-old cathedral pew and prayed for strength.

Never before had redemption felt so close, yet so out of reach. He sucked in a lungful of air, trying to stifle the wave of loneliness that swept through him. If only Rufina could see him now, she'd realize how he suffered.

Just be quiet until she leaves, his brain said.

"You look like you've been out having fun," his big mouth said.

Isabella jumped and spun to face him, the motion causing her dress to shimmer in the half-light. Her hand instantly went to her breast, above which dangled a priceless diamond necklace. "Nick! You scared me to death!"

"I'm sorry. I did warn you that I like to work at all hours." He walked closer, knowing he should have kept silent, but controlled by the pull he'd felt since their first meeting. He gestured to the dress and the diamonds encircling her throat. "Been to a party?"

"A benefit dinner."

"Must have had a good time, if you're just finishing up now." For a moment, he wondered if her voice had been among the dozens he'd heard emanating from the garden. Had she met a clandestine lover under the rose arbor? Flirted with a young aristocrat in the moonlight? Despite her obvious sex appeal, for some reason, he doubted it. The princess didn't seem the type to engage in secret rendezvous.

Isabella leaned back against the desk, her toes poking out from under her dress to reveal moccasin-style slippers. "It was a successful event," she finally answered, then covered her mouth to hide a yawn. "We raised over half a million San Riminian draema for the Red Cross. They'll use the money from tonight's dinner to further their work in the Balkans."

Nope. Definitely no tête-à-tête in the garden for the princess tonight.

"Don't get too excited, Your Highness," he joked.

He could tell the Red Cross's mission meant a great deal to her, but her eyes lacked the spark he'd seen when she'd spoken of her mother's museum project. Or Federico's children. If she'd spent the night flirting with a lover, he'd have seen it in her eyes.

She let out a small laugh. "No matter how glittery and exciting these events might seem, they run together in my head after awhile. I know the causes are important, and that my presence can make a great difference to an organization in need of funds, but for the last year or two, I've gone through them on auto-pilot. I show up, I say something meaningful, I shake all the right hands, then run back to my secretary so I can gear up for the next one." Her words came out accented, spoken like most San Riminians who'd learned English as a second language, as opposed to the near-perfect American English she usually used.

She gasped, then put a hand to her lips. "I can't believe I just said that. Please, please, forget what I said. I'm overtired."

He frowned. "Have you slept since we arrived back?"

She shook her head.

"What about on the flight? I know I was out like a light."

She shifted her rear on the desk. "No, not really."

"Then why in the world are you down here?" He jabbed a finger toward the door. "Go to bed, Your Highness!" Not that he wanted her to leave, but if ever a person needed a vacation, even for a few hours, it was Isabella diTalora. Besides, he needed to stop staring at her in that dress, and he found it physically impossible while she was in the room.

A smile tugged at the corner of her mouth. "And here I thought I'd gotten you to Princess."

He laughed aloud. She might be tired, but she still had her wit. "Fine. Go to bed, Princess."

"I will. But to answer your question," she twisted on the desk, indicating a rolled-up piece of paper he hadn't noticed, "I brought you the chart you'd asked Nerina about."

"Couldn't wait until morning?"

Her shoulders, bare except for two spaghetti-thin silver straps, lifted a notch. "I have an engagement in the morning. I was afraid I might not make it down here until later." She raised her shapely rear from the desk, but kept her eyes averted from his. Tilting her head toward the back of the room, she asked, "Have you found anything else exciting? Besides the sword, I mean?"

Yes, you. "I'm still getting the lay of the land."

She finally lifted her gaze to his, all business once again. "Well, then, the chart should help. I might not be down here for a few days, so if you need anything as you get started, please let Nerina know. If there's anything that needs to be relayed to the museum board—"

"Why do you do it?"

She blinked. "Do what?"

"All of it." He swept a hand in the direction of the main palace. "You haven't slept in I don't know how long, you bust your tail raising money for charitable causes, then schedule some engagement for bright and early tomorrow morning despite knowing that you'd have had an overnight flight the day before. You personally decide to oversee my work, though you could have appointed someone else and made life a lot easier on yourself. And on top of all that, you seem to be the official palace mother hen, watching over everyone in this household to make sure they're happy. Why do you do it?''

She stared at him in silence. He thought for a moment she'd walk out, incensed at his forthright—and probably disrespectful—analysis of her personality. But then something softened in her gaze. ''I do it because I can. And because I want to.''

She shook her head slowly, causing a few tendrils of hair to fall against her nape. ''You know, most little girls dream of becoming a princess. They dress up and pretend that it's all parties and chivalrous knights coming to sweep them away. Reality is different. Being a princess in today's world brings with it a lot of responsibility. People rely on you, people you love. And even if your feet ache and you can barely hold your head up you're so exhausted, something in here,'' she tapped her chest, ''makes you go on. Because you know that what you do makes a difference for hundreds, maybe even thousands, of those people.''

''But you can't help them if you're so tired you can barely stand,'' he argued.

''If you love someone with all your heart, you won't let them down. No matter how tired you are, no matter what personal sacrifices you might have to make. And I love my country and my family with all my heart.'' Her face lit up as she spoke, and again she reminded him of an angel, with her shimmering silver gown trailing to the floor. ''I can't help it.''

Before he could think better of it, he reached out to her, tucking a loose strand of hair behind her ear. For a woman who spent so much time traveling the world, meeting dignitaries and hobnobbing with the upper crust, she possessed a purity of spirit that surprised him. She'd been quick to put him in his place when she'd visited his office, so he knew she had a sharp mind and the ability to assess a situation and adapt. And she'd read him well enough at their very first meeting to entice him into coming to San Rimini, despite his initial misgivings.

But despite her intellect, and despite her uncanny ability to understand people's basic nature, she still believed she could change the world.

''Life is short,'' he said, his voice coming out in a whisper. ''You are so beautiful, so intelligent. And you give to so many people. Don't forget to take time for yourself.''

He allowed his fingers to trail down her cheek. She stood immobile, her soft brown eyes allowing him to see into her soul. He understood her need to give to others. He'd fought dozens of battles and given himself without question to King Bernardo's service to make a better life for himself and Coletta. But completely denying one's personal desires and needs…he'd given up on that notion long ago. Years of ''sacrifice'' taught him the hard way that any differences one made would be small, or fleeting, at best.

''What I do makes me happy.'' Her voice came out

as a plea, as if a silent battle waged within her at his words. Or perhaps at his touch.

"But giving so much of yourself also makes you lonely. Doesn't it?"

The realization struck him even as he said the words. The world's most famous princess, the woman the tabloids chased and the fashion magazines praised, lived a solitary existence. He tried to recall the press about her. Had she dated anyone? Been caught kissing anyone by a well-positioned telephoto lens? He could recall stories about her brothers—Antony being called the Playboy Prince for a brief time, Stefano carousing about Europe with voluptuous women on each arm, Federico marrying the wealthy, elegant Lady Lucrezia—but nothing about Isabella.

"No," she argued, but to his ears, the words came out sounding like she wanted to convince herself more than him. "I'm never lonely. I have an incredible family. My father and I get along wonderfully, and—"

"It's not the same, is it?"

The question hung in the air for a split second before he saw the truth in her eyes. Without waiting for her denial, he lowered his head to hers, brushing her lips with the most gentle, chaste kiss he could ever remember giving a woman.

Yet he'd never wanted a woman more.

"Perhaps you should go to sleep now, Princess," he managed as he pulled away. "The least you deserve for your hard work is a few hours rest."

Besides, between the sword incident this afternoon and their intimate exchange now, his desire had built itself to near-fever pitch. If she stayed in the storeroom one moment longer, he might not be able to stop himself from easing those silvery straps off her shoulders and showing her just how lonely she'd become.

But if he wanted to keep his mind on his job, and on finding Rufina, he couldn't allow himself to take what his body craved, or give Isabella what she so desperately needed.

For until he found Rufina, he could give himself to no one. He'd made that promise the day he lost Coletta.

Isabella's sweet eyes misted for a moment, then she dropped her gaze from his. "You're right. I need to get to sleep."

She scooted away from his touch, and he sensed her reluctance at parting was nearly as strong as his own. The beginnings of another headache crept into his skull, so he grabbed his aspirin bottle from the desk and popped two into his mouth. At the sound of the desk drawer opening, Isabella paused at the bottom of the steps, and her hand trailed along the doorframe for a moment, as if she was gathering her thoughts.

She turned to him, her silky voice returning to its usual accent-free tone. "As I said, I'll be busy for the next few days. If you need anything, please let Nerina know. You might want to ask her for an appointment calendar, if you haven't already. My next meeting with the museum board is in two weeks, and I'd like to have a full report of your work-in-progress to present to them."

She frowned then, looking at the aspirin bottle in his hand. "Are you all right, Nick?"

He nodded. "I had a head injury once, so I get a lot of headaches. Don't read anything into it."

She looked from the aspirin bottle to him, then without saying a word, she disappeared into the hallway. He stood by the door, listening to her soft slippers patter against the floor, first at a walk, then at a jog.

He closed his eyes for a moment, wishing her out of his aching head, then turned and strode back to the crates.

Only Rufina could save him now.

Chapter Five

Isabella plucked a black Montegrappa fountain pen from the walnut pencil cup on her desk, then began sifting through the stack of correspondence filling her in-box. Eight invitations to answer, thirty-six thank-you notes to dictate and letters from the German chancellor and Italian prime minister to respond to.

Nerina better warm up the coffeepot again.

According to the morning schedule Nerina left on her desk, after the correspondence was complete Isabella had a series of dress fittings with a representative from Giorgio Armani, who'd lobbied to outfit her for the Venice Film Festival. Once he was safely off the palace grounds, Isabella had arranged private fittings for two Versace gowns, one for a charity ball sponsoring the San Riminian Scholarship Fund, which was her brother Antony's pet project, and one for a dinner honoring San Rimini's recent Nobel Prize-winning chemist.

Though having high-end designers stick her with pins and cluck about how they might hide her figure flaws wasn't Isabella's idea of a good time, unfortunately, it came with the princess job description.

Over Isabella's shoulder, Nerina pecked away at her computer keyboard. Though the grandfather clock in the princess's small palace office chimed 7:30 a.m., they'd been working for over an hour, and Isabella had already finished her second cup of coffee.

She glanced once more at the schedule. Nothing on the list that would take her near the keep. Though she couldn't put off facing him forever, she'd successfully avoided Nick for nearly two weeks. True, the three-day trip she'd taken to Berlin to attend a conference on the worldwide refugee crisis helped. But the rest of the time, she'd steered clear of the storeroom and the area near his guest rooms out of sheer determination.

Even so, as Isabella slit open an engraved dinner invitation and realized it came from the Italian banker who'd monopolized her time at the Red Cross benefit dinner, an image of Nick immediately filled her mind. She could picture the planes of his face, the dark mystique of his eyes, the warmth of his skin as if he stood only inches away. And then there was his kiss, so tender, yet obviously wanting more.

And she'd been more than ready to give it, despite years of avoiding relationships.

What in the world is wrong with me? She examined the invitation again. Dozens of successful, good-looking men pursued her—men like the Italian banker—who came from good families, wealthy families. It was all part and parcel of being a young royal.

She'd been able to dismiss them easily enough, but for a reason she couldn't identify, Nick captured her interest in a way no man had before. And, she admitted, he'd captured her desire. How many nights during the past two weeks had she lain awake at night, wondering if he was in the storeroom? Wondering what might happen if she allowed herself to wander down there again?

And how often had she caught herself pondering his words? He was wrong, of course. How could someone who never had a moment to herself possibly be lonely?

"Your Highness, how would you like to handle Mr. Black?"

Isabella's head snapped up, and she realized she'd stopped sorting the correspondence while daydreaming about Nick.

"Handle him?"

"You must not have gotten to it yet." Nerina gestured toward the paper pile on Isabella's desk. "He has been sending his research notes to his secretary in Boston for transcription, and has had her do any Internet searches he's required. However, he feels he could work more efficiently if he had a computer and Internet access himself."

Isabella frowned. "I thought I'd allocated plenty of money for that."

Nerina's head dipped, showing the same quiet respect for the princess as she always had for her last employer, Queen Aletta. "You did, Your Highness. However, Mr. Black has requested a computer setup for the storeroom, as opposed to using facilities which already exist in the main palace. I'm afraid the keep isn't adequately wired.''

"No, it's not. The maintenance staff complains that the power gets shorted out down there all the time. I doubt it could support two hair dryers going at once, let alone a computer and all the peripherals.''

"That's what I told Mr. Black, but he insisted, so I checked further.''

"And?''

"Maintenance explained that we'd have to call in an outside electrician, which is simple enough, but you'll need your father's permission and a waiver from the San Riminian Historical Council first, since the keep falls under San Rimini's historic preservation laws.''

"Father wouldn't be a problem.'' The Council would be another matter, and they both knew it. There had been a five-year fight before the renovation of the guest rooms in the 1960s. And a six-month debate to install a new ventilation system just last year.

"I did offer Mr. Black full, unrestricted use of the library computer and research materials, but he insisted on having a computer in the keep. When I told him that wouldn't be possible, he asked me to refer the matter to you, saying that you would understand his need for complete privacy.''

"Thank you, Nerina. I'll handle it.'' Once she worked up the strength of will to see Nick again. Perhaps in the time that elapsed since their late-night meeting he'd forgotten what passed between them.

Then again, it likely hadn't affected him as it did her.

She turned to her correspondence once again, but

stopped when Nerina added, "While we're on the subject of Mr. Black, your meeting with the museum board is scheduled for three o'clock tomorrow afternoon. The curator has arranged for the lead architect to attend so you can give your final approval to the blueprints. The curator also expects you'll update the board on Mr. Black's progress. When I spoke with Mr. Black about the computer, I reminded him of your meeting."

So much for postponing her return to the storeroom. Now she'd have to talk to Nick. Forcing herself not to sigh aloud, she asked, "Do I have time in my schedule this afternoon to meet with him?"

Nerina pulled a piece of paper from her printer tray, then held it out to the princess. "Your afternoon schedule. I left from three-thirty onward completely open, Your Highness."

The fountain pen fell from Isabella's hand as she read over the sheet of paper. "You're joking."

"I am not." Her secretary's all-business, all-the-time expression gave way to a wide smile. "When you finish with Mr. Black, may I suggest you rest, Your Highness? I will ensure you are not disturbed. Consider it a birthday present."

"It's not...." Isabella's gaze dropped to the small calendar on the corner of her ebony-inlaid cherry desktop. Sure enough, she'd forgotten her own birthday.

"*Sì*. It is."

Isabella leaped up from the desk and embraced Nerina. "*Lei è un santa*, Nerina!"

Nerina blushed with pride. "A saint, no. Tomorrow will be a full day, I fear."

"It doesn't matter. *Grazie.*" With renewed energy, she turned back to the desk, eager to tackle the correspondence. So long as she made it through her meeting with Nick, she'd enjoy the best evening she had in a long, long time. And she'd spend it blissfully alone.

Nick massaged the back of his neck, trying to shake his persistent headache, then returned his attention to the seven-hundred-year-old calfskin-bound book before him. A collection of medieval sermons, written in Latin and with beautiful, still-clear illumination, it would make a wonderful addition to San Rimini's museum. He ran his gloved finger along the edge, wondering if he'd once known the monk who'd labored over it. During his own years in an Italian monastery, he'd transcribed four books. Unfortunately, the time-consuming task brought him no closer to breaking his curse.

When Rufina told him only sacrifice would break the curse, she apparently hadn't meant sacrificing his life to the church. It had taken him nearly fifteen years to figure that one out.

He clicked the red button on his handheld tape recorder, described the book's age, condition and historical importance, then assigned it an item number, which he also logged in a notebook. Tomorrow, he'd have another batch of tapes to send to Anne for transcription.

He scanned the long row of item numbers listed in his notebook. Princess Isabella should be pleased with his progress. If the documents in the rest of the crates proved as promising as the first batch had, the Royal

Museum of San Rimini would have plenty of material to include in an expansion, and he hadn't even begun to catalogue the artifacts crowding the stalls yet. The tapestries and paintings alone might take him a month.

He set down the tape recorder and stretched his legs under the desk. On his own mission, he'd made no progress whatsoever. Most of the scrolls and texts he'd discovered in the storeroom crates were spiritual in nature, which he'd expected. In medieval times, scribes were trained to commit prayers, sermons, choral arrangements and other religious works to paper. Books were expensive to produce and considered works of art, so only religious or scholarly works were seen as worthy of recording. Still, Nick had come across the occasional reference text as well as several scrolls describing significant events in San Rimini's villages. With any luck, he'd find an undiscovered book on witchcraft or a record of witch trials.

Two calls over the past few days to Roger confirmed his fears there—that the texts he'd left Roger to analyze only repeated material Nick had found in dozens of other books and documents on medieval witchcraft over the years, with no references to any suspected witches fitting Rufina's description.

Nick rose from the desk and carried the books he'd analyzed during the early-afternoon hours to a crate of completed materials, then reached into a nearby crate and carefully withdrew three more priceless medieval books. Tonight, perhaps, he'd start on one of the stalls, inspecting the artifacts just to shake up his routine. And to keep his mind off Isabella.

The problem with scouring text after text was that

the mind tended to wander. And of course, his thoughts were never far from a certain princess. Every time he sat at his desk, he envisioned her childlike smile, her smooth olive skin, her fathomless amber eyes. Part of him wished he'd done more than give her a simple kiss, wished he'd taken things to the next level—or as far as she'd have allowed. But the larger part of him knew he'd stepped over the line just by caressing her soft cheek. Admitting that he'd been unable to stop himself from touching her drove him to distraction.

Setting the ancient books back in the open crate, he stripped off his cotton gloves, tossed them on his desk, then crossed the room to the stall Isabella's chart identified as containing items from roughly 1100 to 1250, the years prior to his birth through the Third and Fourth Crusades. He let his gaze wander over the stall's interior, instantly recognizing a half-unrolled, threadbare tapestry. A gift from Philip Augustus of France, it hung in King Bernardo's throne room whenever French dignitaries were in residence—and came down when Richard I and his followers paid a visit. Nick couldn't help but smile in remembrance, despite the fact the tapestry was beyond repair.

Though proper investigative techniques dictated he sort through the crates of documents first, for his own purposes, he probably should have started here. A chest near the stall door opened at the touch of a finger to reveal battered tankards and cooking pots from the kitchens. Behind the chest, a cracked wrought-iron chandelier rested atop a badly rotted trunk. A smith's tools crowded one corner, and a damaged painting rested in another. He could see why these items ended up forgotten beneath the oldest part of the palace for so many centuries. Most were unsalvageable. Still, there were those historians at the museum who'd probably want to study them. He picked his way through the stall, studying the contents, until he spied a box designed to hold documents. He pried off the lid, then selected a fragile scroll from the top. He unrolled it with care, expecting to see a prayer or perhaps an armory inventory, but instead found a hard lump forming in his throat as he read a list of names and notations written in Italian instead of the scholarly Latin. Each man's name brought forth a familiar, but long-dead, face. All were knights promised to Richard the Lionhearted in the Third Crusade. Knights whose names had been listed on the very communiqué he'd been entrusted to carry to Richard where he'd wintered his troops in Sicily in 1190.

And then he saw the name that stopped him cold.

Domenico di Bollazio, primo figlio di Rizardo. Ventisette. Dominic of Bollazio, eldest son of Rizardo. Aged twenty-seven.

His hands shook; an ice-cold sweat covered his skin. He closed his eyes until he could regain his emotional control, then he slowly scanned the rest of the lengthy scroll. Bernardo's name, written in the king's own distinctive hand, was scribbled across the bottom next to his seal.

Oh, yes. He definitely should have started in the stall.

"Excuse me, Nick?"

He spun in the cramped area, nearly dropping the

dried parchment at the sound of Isabella's voice. "Princess."

She looked every bit as beautiful as the night she'd entered the storeroom in her ethereal silver gown and stood in the half-light of the staircase. Today, however, she appeared more down-to-earth, wearing a business-beige pantsuit, a soft ivory blouse and only a hint of makeup. Tasteful diamond stud earrings sparkled in her earlobes and her dark hair draped past her shoulders in long, loose curls.

He realized he'd never seen her with her hair down and thanked God for it. He couldn't have stopped himself the other night if he'd been able to run his fingers through her shiny tresses. He wondered if her curls would feel as silky-soft as her skin had beneath his fingertips.

"I didn't mean to disturb you." She glanced around the stall, studying the dusty artifacts that crammed every available inch of space. "Nerina said you wanted to see me about getting a computer."

Gathering himself, he carefully set the scroll back in the box where he'd found it. As important as such a discovery would be to the museum, and to medieval historians everywhere, it was far more important to him personally. For the time being, he'd keep the scroll to himself.

"Yes." He tried to concentrate on the princess. "I've been dictating my notes and mailing the tapes to Anne, but it would be more efficient if I could simply type them myself."

"I could have Nerina do it."

He shot her a knowing look. "You and I both know she's too busy to tackle my work. She can barely manage to keep up with you. Besides, I'd like computer access so I can scan some of the scrolls I've discovered. My assistant, Roger, has a contact at the University of Kentucky who's digitizing medieval documents. With your permission, I'd like to have him look at a few of these, see if they should be copied to a computer file for preservation and further study before being turned over to the museum.''

''It's going to be tough getting a computer down here, I'm afraid. Historical preservation laws prevent having the keep wired for modern electronics. I'd have to explain to Parliament why I want a waiver. To make their determination, they'd need to look further into your work.''

She rested a shoulder against the stall door and studied him for a moment. ''Keeping the museum board at arm's length is one thing, Parliament's another. I assume you don't want them involved in what you're doing.''

''No.'' He picked up a broken sword tang that had been left lying on a nearby shelf and grasped it hard, so his nervous fingers wouldn't betray him. He'd suspected when Isabella offered him the job that this day would come, when he'd need to risk his privacy to further his research, despite her assurances to the contrary. Still, she'd already done more to guarantee his solitude than he'd expected. ''My only option is the palace library?''

''It's the only computer not already in use. I will do my best to keep the staff away while you're working, but it is in a busy area.''

Parliament or the palace staff. Not the best of choices. His concern must have shown on his face, because the princess added, "I did think of another option. I could fly your secretary here."

He set the tang down beside the document box, thinking over the proposition. At home, Anne generally worked in her office and he worked in his, with the door shut. She didn't monitor his movements or the details of his research. She went home promptly at 5:00 p.m., and never asked questions about his personal life. Living and working within the confines of the keep, she'd soon realize he sought something specific. Still, it was better than the alternatives. And now, inside the document box to his left, he'd finally found a record of his own existence. If he could find his own name, he could surely find Rufina, who'd been notorious at the time. Then privacy might not matter any more.

"It's a very kind offer."

"It's no trouble, really. Especially if it improves the chance you'll have the artifacts analyzed and catalogued in time for the expansion."

He flashed her a smile of gratitude. "I'll let you know."

"Good." She straightened, and her gaze slipped past him, to the jumble of furniture and rolled-up tapestries crowding the far wall of the stall. "I came for another reason, as well. As Nerina must have mentioned, I meet with the museum board tomorrow. They'll expect a full report on your findings."

"I can get that to you tonight, if that works for your schedule."

"Should give me plenty of time to look it over, thank you." Her voice was polite, distant, as if the last time they'd been in this room together hadn't registered. But she shifted from one foot to another, and he guessed their proximity in the isolated room affected her, though she didn't wish to show it.

He wondered if she thought of their kiss as often as he did. He knew why he'd resisted kissing her, but what held *her* back? Why didn't she feel she could enjoy a little comfort in the arms of a man?

"Is there anything else you need?" she asked, taking a step back.

You. "I don't believe so," he answered, matching her formal tone. "Nerina has gone out of her way to make certain I'm accommodated."

"Good," she replied, but once again her gaze flicked past him.

"What are you looking at?" He turned, curious.

"Oh, it's nothing. Just…I thought my mother had all the books put into crates. But I see one was left in here." When he didn't see it right away, she edged into the stall, so close he could breathe in her elegant, feminine perfume. Reaching past him, she lifted a book off a spindly wooden chair. "I can put it with the others, if you'd like."

"Thanks." He gave it a cursory look. From what he could tell of the design, it wasn't the correct era for the stall, anyway. Probably mid-1400s.

The princess ran her small hands over the pigskin-covered wooden boards, admiring the worn thistle-and-leaf design on the cover. "It's beautiful, isn't it?" Her voice came out in a whisper, and he could see from her face how excited the discovery made her. He didn't doubt now that she'd studied art history at Harvard; her interest was apparent from the loving way she held the book. Despite his mind warning him not to draw any closer, not to risk touching her again, he leaned over her shoulder for a better look.

"It has a lock on it," she said, pointing out a blackened hinge covering the book's endpapers. "Could it be a diary? And this metal ring at the top...what was its purpose?"

"I doubt it's a diary." He dipped his head toward it. "May I?"

She held the book out, and he took it from her hands, successfully resisting the urge to caress her fingers with his own. After fiddling with the lock for a few moments, he found the latch to spring it open. "Voilà." The pages crackled despite his care in opening the lock. He handed the book back to her. "For you, Your Highness."

"Isabella."

"Princess." He grinned. "Books were quite valuable in medieval times. Locks were put on the covers to protect the pages from exposure to the elements. And the ring at the top was once connected to a chain."

"I remember reading about those," she said in wonder. "Didn't they chain books to desks to keep them from being stolen from libraries and monasteries? This was how they did it, through this loop?"

"You must have been a good student at Harvard."

"Had to be. Could you imagine what the tabloids would say if a princess flunked out?"

"Royal Bombshell Bombs Out?"

"Very funny."

She studied the pages, then exclaimed, "It's in Latin... It's a book of fairy tales!"

"Fairy tales?"

"From a scholar's point of view, I think." She pointed to a series of words near the top of the open page. "Look. It discusses how fairy tales vary from village to village, but espouse the same morals."

He looked down at her in awe. "You read Latin?" He shook his head. "No, of course you do."

"I'm a bit rusty," she admitted. "But I think this is a description of *Goldilocks and the Three Bears.* See? This word is 'girl' and I think this is talking about the 'house of a bear.' What do you think?"

He took the book back from her, careful not to tear the fragile paper. "You're right."

He turned a few more pages, then laughed aloud. "What do you know? *The Fox and the Grapes.* A different version than I heard growing up, but essentially the same."

"A worthwhile discovery?"

She turned her body just enough to gaze up at him, and once again he was struck by her innocence. Never in a million years had he expected the sophisticated Princess Isabella to be a quiet academic at heart.

"Definitely. Here." He took her hands and placed the book between her palms. "I know it probably should be analyzed by a literature expert, but I think you should take it for yourself."

"Me?"

"It's been down here for ages and no one's missed it. If you kept it, no one would be the wiser."

She turned over the book in her hands. "I couldn't. It belongs to the people of San Rimini, in their museum. It's what my mother would have wanted."

"Your mother would have wanted you to have a birthday present."

He'd promised himself he wouldn't mention it, wouldn't do anything out of the ordinary if he ran into her today. The last thing he wanted was to let on that he had feelings for her, though of course, after two weeks of constantly thinking about her, he knew he did. What red-blooded man wouldn't?

But seeing her reaction to the book made him want to give it to her, resolve be damned. Didn't she deserve a little happiness? A little something for herself?

"Nerina told you," she accused.

"Maybe."

"I need to have a talk with her."

"Not that I'm sticking up for Nerina, mind you," he cocked an eyebrow at her, "because the woman doesn't seem to care much for me or my computer demands. But someone had to say something. Your father and Prince Antony have huge soirées for their birthdays every year. Yet you don't have so much as a tea party planned for yourself, I'm willing to bet."

"Maybe I'm not a big fan of birthday parties."

"Maybe you don't want to bother anyone with planning one for you."

She backed up a step, a difficult feat in the cluttered stall. "I'm not the all-giving saint you think I am. For your information, I'm not doing one single thing for anyone else tonight. No fund-raisers, no state dinners, nothing. I'm treating myself to a night off."

He snorted. "What, sitting at your desk and reading up on world events? Studying your book on independent film? That's not a night off. What about a night out? Don't you want a party?"

"I attend a lot of parties."

"But not parties for *you.* Not parties for fun."

She put up a hand. "Stop. I'm perfectly happy not having a party. It's the last thing I want or need."

"Then how about dinner for two?"

As soon as the words left his mouth, his chest tightened in alarm. What possessed him? He couldn't possibly traipse around town with the princess; his picture would appear in every rag in the Western world within twenty-four hours. Plus, if he'd been tempted to kiss her after a short encounter in a dusty storeroom, what would happen over a plate of pasta and a carafe of Merlot?

Not that she'd accept his offer.

"Are—are you asking me for a date, Mr. Black?" Her face registered shock, but only for a moment, before she regained her ever-present poise.

"It's Nick. Remember, *Princess?*" he joked, hoping to lighten the mood. "And I suppose so." Much as he knew it was a stupid move, he couldn't backpedal now. What kind of jerk rescinded an invitation to a princess? "You wouldn't take the book. Don't you deserve something nice on your birthday?"

"I'm not sure it would be wise. After all, you're on the palace payroll now, and…well, I don't remember the last time I went out on a private date. Something other than a formal event."

He forced himself not to show his relief. His lack of feminine contact—if one didn't count Anne, which he didn't—made him take stupid risks. Now that the danger of a date had passed, however, his curiosity got the better of him. "You can tell me to take a hike, Princess, but why haven't you dated? No available men in San Rimini?"

She bit her bottom lip, unable to hide her smile. "No, plenty of them. All Stefano's friends, as a matter of fact. And even a few of Antony and Federico's."

"Then?"

She rolled her eyes, a particularly unroyal reaction he found amusing. "I'm the only female in my family. It changes things for me. When the tabloids covered my brothers' romantic interests, for instance, they mostly discussed which women they dated, where they went, things like that. But when it comes to my private life, they've been downright nasty. They insinuate that since I'm a woman, I should keep to a higher standard. Be more circumspect." Isabella puffed out a frustrated breath. "My mother warned me that San Rimini's traditional ways are still revered by many of our subjects, particularly where women are concerned, but I didn't listen. What teenager would? But it turned out she was right."

Before he could stop himself, Nick closed the distance between them and put his hand on her shoulder. Even through the fabric of her suit, he could feel the delicate curve of her collarbone, and he caressed it with his thumb. "Was it really that bad?"

"I shouldn't be talking to you about this." She hesitated, and Nick thought she'd ask him to move his hand or make some excuse to leave, but instead, she met his gaze with gratitude.

"I went out on my first unaccompanied date during my freshman year at Harvard. A nice sophomore I'd met in the library. Just one date, for dinner and a movie in Cambridge. Not even a good-night kiss. Well, not a *real* one, if you know what I mean."

He forced himself not to laugh at the fiery red color creeping across her cheeks. "I know what you mean. So what happened?"

"For the next week, tabloid reporters followed him all over campus, trying to rat out anything negative about him. Turns out that someone living in his residential college got caught smoking pot that same week. The papers made it appear that because they lived in the same building, he must also be a pothead and therefore I was an embarrassment to my country."

He continued to massage her shoulder through her soft suit jacket. "That's terrible. And so unfair."

"It was," she acknowledged, though her voice held no regret, only an understanding that came with time and maturity. "He had no interest in seeing me again after that, and I can't blame him. He planned to attend law school and feared it would hurt his chances. After that, I had no interest in dating again, either. Given what the tabloids might dig up, it's been easier not to date at all."

"You don't miss it?" he asked. He certainly did. He couldn't imagine that a woman with Isabella's compassion and capability for love would willingly relinquish herself to the same hell on earth he faced. No wonder she'd been emotional as they'd rolled down the runway in Boston. The city held a lot of memories for her.

She shook her head no, but he could see from her expression it wasn't the truth. "I'm so busy I don't have time to miss it. And it's not as if I don't meet men at palace events or in the course of my work. I do date, I suppose. It's just a different kind of dating." She raised a finger in warning, and a smile curved her lips, instantly lightening the mood. "So don't accuse me of being lonely again."

"Sounds lonely to me. But if you're commanding me not to argue, I won't." He hated to see her missing out on what could be a fantastic life, filled with all the love she deserved.

"Tell you what." She laughed. "If you can figure out how to keep the reporters away, I'll take you up on your offer. I don't have anything planned tonight, and I can think of nothing I'd like more than to prove you wrong."

Now it was his turn to register shock. His hand stilled on her shoulder. "You want to go out to dinner with me?"

"Yes. If tonight's good. As you said, I deserve it."

Her eyes held an adventurous spark he couldn't resist. "Okay, Princess, if that's what you want, that's what you'll get. Here's how we're going to do it."

Chapter Six

"That's the most casual outfit you own?"

Isabella tugged at the hem of her short-sleeved lilac sweater, which topped a pair of black capri pants and simple flats she'd pulled from the very back of her closet. "It's what I wear when I'm at our country house. And only then on days when no media access is granted. I'm afraid it's as casual as I get."

Nick had promised to help disguise her, and once she'd accepted his dinner invitation, he'd sent her back to her apartments with instructions to put her hair in a ponytail—a style she never wore—and dress down as much as she could before dinner.

"No ripped jeans? Ugly sweatshirts?" he teased. "No, of course not. Do you at least own a pair of sunglasses?"

"At night? That'd be obvious, wouldn't it?"

He glanced at the small window above the desk. "Right. Been on the lower level so long I forget what time of day it is.'' He studied her for a moment, his forehead creased in thought. ''To pull this off, you need to dress in such a way that even if someone thinks you look just like Princess Isabella, they'll automatically assume that you couldn't possibly be her.''

''Trust me, no one will believe *this* is me.'' At least she hoped not.

Nick shook his head in disagreement. ''Maybe some reading glasses? Something you're not photographed in?''

The last thing she wanted Nick to see her wearing. Not that it should matter. ''I have a pair in my purse. But they're ghastly.''

''Put 'em on, Princess.''

She smiled to herself as she pulled out the leather case. What was it about Nick Black that made her heart leap? Certainly no one spoke to her as he did; it was as if he knew a hundred princesses and spoke to them every day. Formal enough to show respect, yet relaxed enough to make her feel like a real person, someone who could hang out in a restaurant with a bunch of other twenty- and thirty-somethings, maybe slouch in her chair and have a beer without raising eyebrows.

Okay, so she wouldn't slouch. Or have a beer. But hanging out with people her own age, without worrying about whether she'd arrive late for her next appointment or be questioned by reporters who hung on her every word, sounded heavenly. And with Nick, it felt possible.

''I wouldn't call them ghastly,'' he said once she had the black-rimmed glasses on. He met her gaze, assessing her disguise. His perusal sent a shiver of excitement through her. It was a huge risk, going out with Nick, knowing how attractive she found him. But today was her birthday. If ever she deserved to indulge in a little fantasy, a little adventure, it was today. Hopefully, no one would ever know. And if the tabloids did discover her, she'd just say she was conferring with an expert on a project for the museum. Surely that was boring enough not to warrant coverage.

"Well, I feel ghastly," she said as she slipped the now-empty leather case back into her purse. "None of the restaurants I frequent would seat me dressed like this."

"We'll be sure to avoid restaurants you frequent, then." He strode past her, searching around the desk area. Finally, he pulled open one of the lower drawers and withdrew a baseball hat. "Here we go. Wear this. I have a backpack I can put on. If you have one, you should take it instead of your purse."

"Why in the world would I own a backpack?" She eyed the gray ball cap with the red and navy Red Sox logo. "You're serious, aren't you?"

He waved a hand at his own attire. While she'd been searching for casual clothes in her apartments, he'd changed into a pair of clean blue jeans, a short-sleeved black T-shirt and black loafers. "We'll look like grad students, especially if we eat somewhere near the University of San Rimini. It's only a mile or so away. With the backpacks on, no one will give us a second look."

"Okay." She put the hat on, pulling her ponytail

through the back. "But I look like an American teen-ager, and I *feel* like a fashion don't."

He laughed. "You actually look quite pretty. And very young."

She felt her cheeks redden, and thanked him for the compliment before adding, "Let's leave before you try to transform me any further."

He picked up a backpack he'd left lying near the desk, looped it over his shoulders, then started walking toward the door. "One problem," he muttered, turning around. "Any idea how we can get out of here? If we go strolling out the gates, we'll be sunk before we even start. There must be a number of journalists assigned to watch the palace."

"Here." She grabbed his hand, pulling him through the open boxes and crates toward the back of the storeroom, feeling remarkably like the adventurous young student she pretended to be. Soon, they were facing the rear wall. She let go of his fingers, then used her hands to feel along the stones. It didn't take long to find the correct stone and the latch hidden behind it.

"What is that?" Nick leaned forward to study the wall.

"Would you believe a secret passage? My grandfather had it constructed during World War II. We hid the crown jewels and most of our valuables in here at the beginning of the war. Lucky for us, the Nazis only occupied San Rimini for a short time before the war started going badly for them and they transferred most of their soldiers to other fronts. But while they were here, my grandfather moved the Jewish members of his staff and their families to the keep, where they'd have easy access to the passage so they could escape or at least hide if the Nazis ever seized control of the palace."

"But that never happened."

"Luckily, no. My grandfather couldn't leave the grounds, but the Nazis didn't enter, either."

She fidgeted with the latch for a moment before it opened, causing a section of the stone wall to move. Nick grunted in surprise when he realized that the stones covering the entrance concealed a reinforced steel door with a numerical keypad on the front.

"Eleven, twenty-two, thirty-seven," Isabella said over her shoulder as she punched in the combination. "The date of my grandfather's coronation."

"The Nazis wouldn't have guessed that?"

She laughed, and Nick reveled in the fact he'd been the one to make her so relaxed and happy. "The code was changed daily during the war, so no. When my father was crowned, Antony was still a teenager and my father was desperately trying to drill important dates in San Rimini's history into his head. He figured that by setting the code to his own father's coronation date, Antony would be less likely to forget it. We've left it that way ever since."

The door swung open, and Isabella waved for Nick to enter the dark corridor behind her. Once they were inside with the door closed, she reached to her left and flipped a switch, illuminating a series of lights along the ceiling. The passage was narrow, apparently built in haste. Overhead support beams stretched in front of him as far as he could see. Plywood cabinets which Nick guessed once held the family's treasures extended from the walls to about hip-height, and rows of empty shelves stood above the cabinet doors.

Isabella followed his gaze. "My grandfather had those filled with canned goods, flashlights, blankets and radios. There's even a small commode farther down. Just in case."

"He was a good king." He remembered King Alberto's defiance in the face of the Nazi occupation, and the worldwide outpouring of support for the brave San Riminians. Now that he'd met Isabella, he decided she'd inherited her grandfather's strength of mind. Had she faced the Nazis, he imagined she'd have shown the same fortitude as the late king.

"That's what my father says," she agreed. "I should have mentioned the corridor to you earlier, but it slipped my mind. It's been ages since I've been down here."

"No reason I'd have to know." Nick adjusted his backpack on his shoulders as they began walking side-by-side through the narrow passage. Every so often their arms brushed against each other, but Isabella didn't shy away from the contact.

The princess raised an eyebrow at him. "You wouldn't think so if you'd been working away cataloguing artifacts in the middle of the night and Stefano came up behind you."

"He uses this passageway?"

"All the time. Well, before he met his fiancée, at least. He'd sneak out with his friends and go hiking or skiing when he should have been attending palace events. It frustrated my father to no end. Antony, Federico and I had to make excuses for Stef on more than one occasion."

All the more reason Princess Isabella felt obliged to stay close to home and fulfill her duties, Nick guessed, especially once King Eduardo became a widower and her other brothers married.

They walked in silence for some time before Nick spotted something long and lean propped against one wall of the passage. Isabella made a face when they reached the tall black canvas bag.

"Stef's ski equipment," she said in amusement. "Old habits must die hard."

Nick reached up to dust away a spiderweb which strung from the ceiling down to the top of the ski bag. "They haven't been used in a while. The first ski resorts will open in a month or so. If he's planning a getaway, he hasn't taken his skis to be waxed yet."

Isabella turned her face to him. "You're quite observant, you know."

"It's my job."

She smiled at that, but said nothing as they continued down the passage.

"So where does this come out?" Nick finally asked.

"I'll show you. We're almost there." Within minutes, they rounded a corner to face another steel door. Isabella turned a large handle to swing it open, and Nick found himself face-to-face with rows of rolling metal bakers' racks and the overwhelming smell of yeast.

"Here we are," she waved a hand around the room, "the back room of Alessandro's Bakery, on the Strada il Reggiménto."

Regiment Street. Nick couldn't believe it. The very street where he and the other knights listed on the scroll were housed in the early days of the Third Crusade, while they awaited their marching orders from King Bernardo. It occurred to him that Bernardo would have coveted the passageway that now connected the Strada il Reggiménto to the palace basement, which had served as the long-dead king's armory. Nick could just picture Bernardo plotting how best to use the passageway to surprise his enemies.

Or to spy on his own knights in their quarters and assess their loyalty to the crown.

He and Isabella made their way past rows of ovens and glass-topped refrigerator cases, then through a room containing shelved boxes of sesame seeds, caraway, baking powder, cocoa and bag after bag of flour and sugar, all arranged in neat stacks along the sides of the tile-floored storeroom. The smells reminded him of the old bakery that stood adjacent to the knight's quarters, and though many, many lifetimes had passed, he couldn't help but believe he'd come full circle. Here he was again, on the Strada il Reggiménto, with his fate dependent on the palace, just a quarter mile away.

Isabella's soft voice cut through his thoughts. "The owners are longtime friends of our family," she explained, dodging around a bin full of bagged day-old bread as she led him to the front of the shop. "Besides my family, and perhaps a few descendants of my grandfather's staff, they're the only ones who know of the passageway's existence. Now let's hope—" She stood on her tiptoes and stretched her body so she could run her fingers along the top of the door frame. "Good. Still here." She turned and held up a key. "This wouldn't have been a very long outing if I couldn't get us out of the shop."

She opened the glass door to a pull-down metal gate and knelt to insert the key. He helped her lift the gate, then pull it back down and lock it behind them.

They stood on the sidewalk, which separated the cobblestoned street from dozens of storefronts, most of which were closed for the evening. A bus stop bench across the street seated four women, all carrying shopping bags. Behind the women, a wrought-iron fence bordering the palace gardens allowed passersby to peek through at hundreds of rose beds, each surrounded by boxwood and highlighted from beneath by thousands of tiny white lights. Several people walked by at a quick clip, eager to get home to loved ones. A man on a bicycle passed, bumping along on the cobblestoned street, then looked back at them over his shoulder.

Nick heard Isabella's sharp intake of breath.

"He didn't recognize you."

"I'm glad you're so certain."

"No one expects you to be here, and certainly not dressed as you are. C'mon." He took her hand, weaving his fingers into hers and discovering they fit together as naturally as if they walked hand in hand every day. "Let's find someplace quiet where *you* can people watch for a change."

"Now that," her face broke into a smile that any photographer would have recognized as being distinctly hers, "would be the best birthday present I've ever received."

"Do you realize," Isabella laid her fork across her plate and allowed the waiter to take it away, "I tried on at least thirty different dresses this morning for events I'm scheduled to attend over the next six weeks? Now none of them will fit. I should have had a salad and a plain chicken breast.''

She meant it, too. Never in her life had she eaten with such gusto—minestrone, lasagna verdi, two pieces of bruschetta, two glasses of Chianti—she'd be spending any free time she had during the next week in the palace gym paying for it. If she found the strength to move from the table.

''You didn't have a choice. Liberating, isn't it?''

She smiled at Nick again. Had she stopped smiling all night? ''You know, it is. I may have even burped once or twice.''

Now it was Nick's turn to smile, and her heart beat faster in response. He'd given her the most fabulous night of her life. They'd enjoyed nearly two hours of carefree conversation, talking about everything from the artifacts in the palace basement to Harvard's ice hockey team to the merits of various restaurants in Boston's Italian North End. They discovered their shared madness for Mike's Pastry, an Italian bakery on Hanover Street, though they disagreed about which delivery service boasted the tastiest pizza.

Best of all, for the first time since she'd lived in Boston as a student, and for the first time since her mother died, Isabella felt young. Unburdened. If only for a few hours, she had no schedule to follow, no speeches to give, no appearances to make. As Nick said, she'd been liberated. Not even the waiter, who'd looked straight into her eyes while taking her order, had recognized her.

Nick had even been bold enough to choose an out-door table at a restaurant in the University district, on a hill overlooking the glitzy Strada il Teatro with its endless casinos and theaters. Beyond that, the glori-ous Palazzo d'Avorio, a five-hundred-year-old re-stored fortress, overlooked San Rimini Bay and the Adriatic Sea beyond. Couples laughed and shared se-crets at tables nearby, and well-dressed tourists strolled along the cobblestoned street, pointing out the sights below and discussing their strategies for win-ning big at the blackjack and craps tables.

"Beautiful night, isn't it?" She swirled her Chianti, took a long, slow sip, then breathed in deeply, as if by pulling the sea-scented air into her lungs she could keep it there forever and preserve the night's magic. "This is what I love about my country."

"Even though you don't get to enjoy it yourself?"

"Oh, I do. Just not alone." She glanced across the table at Nick. "Well, you know what I mean."

"I do."

Changing the subject, she tipped her head forward, toward the sea. "It's such a clear night, you can see Venice. See all those lights across San Rimini Bay?"

He turned to look, and nodded. "Nice now, to look across there and see them. Not so nice when the Doges were in power, constantly trying to conquer San Rimini and bring it under Venetian control. I can only imagine what the old kings thought, looking out from the keep and realizing that the enemy was within eyesight at all times."

"Do you ever take off your historian's hat?"

"Guess not." He shrugged, and though there was a half grin on his face, Isabella sensed she'd touched on a deep internal sadness with the question. For the life of her, however, she couldn't figure out why.

The waiter interrupted then, handing them each small leather-bound menus with the evening's dessert selections. Nick ordered tiramisu and black coffee, but Isabella shook her head.

Nick looked at the waiter but jerked his head toward her. *"Zuccotto e cappuccino decaffeinato."*

"Nick—"

He waved the waiter off. *"Grazie."*

"Sometimes I hate that male chauvinism is still tolerated in this country," she protested. "My opinion should count for something here."

"Not where dessert's concerned, no."

"But sponge cake with cream and chocolate? *And* a cappuccino? I'll have a sugar crash just when I'm supposed to meet with the museum board tomorrow. Don't you want me to be at my best?"

"I want you to enjoy your birthday."

When their desserts arrived a few minutes later, he reached across the table and covered her hand with his, preventing her from taking a bite. "Blow out the candle, first, Princess," he urged, nodding toward the dripping candle stuck in an old Chianti bottle on the edge of their table. "Make a wish."

"You're not supposed to blow out table candles," she hissed. "It ruins the ambience of the restaurant, and the waiter would have to—"

He pinned her with a stare. "Just blow out the candle. And don't forget to make a wish."

Opting not to argue, she closed her eyes for a moment, trying to shut out Nick and all the things her soul wished for—for her freedom to last, for the opportunity to experience life like this every night, with a handsome man who cared about her well-being and didn't mind seeing her dressed in shabby clothes and wearing her reading glasses.

For a chance at love, like her parents had shared.

Instead, she forced her thoughts to home, and wished for Federico's heart to heal. She leaned forward and opened her mouth in an *O*.

"No fair wishing for other people, Princess." Nick's whispered voice invaded her thoughts. "Make a wish for yourself. Just this once."

She opened her eyes and caught Nick's dark, knowing eyes fixed upon her face. In that instant, she wished for love, then before she could reconsider she blew out the candle, casting their table in darkness.

"You're very kind to me, Nick Black," she whispered. He still held her right hand in his left on the tabletop, and she reached out with her other hand to cover the scars his bore. He understood her so well, yet she knew so little about him. "You encourage me to go out, to enjoy myself. You seem to thrill to all of life's little pleasures, yet you deny yourself everything. You hide from the public, and you live the life of a hermit. Why?"

His eyes clouded. Even in the dark night, she could see something inside him close off from her. "It's a long story, Princess."

"I have time."

"This story takes more time than anyone on Earth has to hear it." He squeezed her hand, but she didn't feel reassured. "All that matters is that you care enough to ask. Thank you for that." He withdrew his hand from hers and picked up his Chianti glass. "Enjoy your *zuccotto*. We should get back to the palace before long. If we're seen entering the bakery too late someone is liable to think it's a break-in and call the *polizia*."

He took a sip of his Chianti, then focused on his dessert, making it clear the topic was closed. When the waiter returned with the bill, she let Nick pay it, despite her inclination to argue.

"Tell me, Princess," he finally broke the silence as they walked hand in hand back toward the bakery, "what's your favorite childhood memory?"

She cocked an eyebrow at him. "Are you serious?"

"Completely. I need to know that you had fun at some point in your life."

She punched his arm with her free hand, something she hadn't done to anyone but her brothers. "For such a nice guy, you're awfully rotten."

"You're assuming I'm a nice guy."

She laughed, then stared up at the stars as they wound their way back toward the palace, turning from one small street to another as she tried to decide which memory was her most treasured. "I would say listening to my mother read aloud to Stefano and me when we were children. Antony is six years older than I am, and Federico's four years older, but they would even come and hop up on my bed sometimes to hear her read. They didn't seem to mind listening to the same fairy tales over and over again." Tears sprung to her eyes at the memory. "I think they had Mother snowed. As soon as she left for her own room, they'd turn on flashlights under their sheets and read the Hardy Boys books she'd brought them from her trips to the United States. She was so thrilled they wanted to hear her read she never suspected they didn't go right to sleep like they were supposed to. Until our nanny caught them at it, anyway.''

"You really should consider taking the fairy-tale book, Princess."

"Maybe I will."

They let the conversation die, enjoying the sounds of the night, stopping every so often to comment on the storefronts or the architecture of San Rimini's old buildings. The bells of the Duomo tolled the hour, reminding Isabella that her fantasy night would soon come to an end.

"Did your mother read you fairy tales?" she asked.

"She couldn't read." Nick's words were quiet, wistful. "But she told some wonderful stories, yes."

"Is she still alive?"

He shook his head. "No. She died a long time ago."

"But you still miss her."

"Of course I do. I can still hear her voice inside my head, telling me stories of ancient Arabia. Very dark tales, but she made them fascinating."

"Was she from the Middle East?" It would explain his dark coloring, she thought, though she'd assumed when they'd met in his Boston office that he might be of San Riminian descent.

He laughed at that. "No. Believe it or not, she was San Riminian. But my father traveled to the Middle East. She told the tales to pass the time while he was away, I think." He turned to her. "What was your favorite fairy tale?"

"Hmm. Maybe *The Lion and the Mouse.* Or *The*

Elves and the Shoemaker. I don't know. I liked so many—*The Emperor's New Clothes, The Cursed Knight, The Frog Prince*—''

Nick stopped walking. ''The Cursed Knight? I—I haven't heard of that one. What's it about?''

''I thought all San Riminian kids heard that one. You probably just forgot it.''

He pulled her toward a bus stop bench, and she realized that while they'd been talking, she'd lost track of their location. The wrought-iron fence surrounding the palace rose from the sidewalk behind the bench, and the Alessandro family's bakery stood just across the street.

Nick took off his backpack and slung it over the back of the bench, then took a seat and patted the space next to him. ''Tell me. Jog my memory.''

Isabella paused, then took the seat. ''It was about a knight who lived long ago. His ambition ruled his life. He would do anything to gain land for his family and to become important in the eyes of the king.''

Nick's gaze darkened. ''Go on.''

She frowned, feeling silly telling a grown man a fairy tale. ''Well, one day the king sent the knight on an important mission, to deliver a message to another king. As the knight rode his horse through the forest, he came upon a boy in trouble. The boy was trapped underneath a collapsed bridge, and the water beneath the bridge was rising fast—''

''A collapsed bridge? Are you sure?''

''I'm positive. Besides, I thought you said you didn't know this tale.''

''I don't.'' He waved for her to continue. ''My apologies, Princess.''

"Well, the boy cried out to the knight to save him. But the knight was afraid that if he didn't hurry, the message would get to the other king too late, and he would fall out of favor with the king. So he rode on, promising to send back help. As he continued his ride, he came across the boy's mother, who was wandering through the forest looking for him. The knight told the mother where the boy was, and she ran to help him."

"Did she save the boy?" Isabella swallowed at the seriousness of Nick's tone. It was as if he thought the story was real, and the boy's life actually hung in the balance.

"She did, but barely. She was a witch, and used a magic spell to keep him alive. When the knight came through that same area of the forest on his way back to his own lands, she cursed him. She told him that his ambition blinded him to the value of life. Until he could sacrifice his ambition for the needs of another person, he would be cursed to immortality. Since he never aged, he was treated like a pariah from that day forward."

Nick stared ahead into the night. "You were right, Princess. I have heard that tale. But I can't remember what happened to the knight. Did he ever break the curse?"

She shrugged. "I don't know."

"That's unfortunate. I'd be interested to know if the knight ever learned his lesson."

"Well, my nanny told a different version than what I heard in school. According to her, after the knight was cursed, he decided to give up his position at court to his younger brother. He'd always treated his

younger brother badly, and so he thought by sacrificing everything he'd worked for, he'd break the curse.
As it turned out, the younger brother saved the country from a terrible invader, and the king was so grate-
ful he offered the younger knight his daughter's hand
in marriage. The older knight lived a long and happy
life in the country, thankful that his brother had become so successful. The curse never came true.''

Isabella couldn't help but laugh as a thought occurred to her. ''I never realized it before, but I bet
my nanny made that up just to get Antony to be nicer
to Federico and Stefano. He used to pick on them,
especially Federico. He thought he was superior to
them since he was the crown prince. Leave it to my
old nanny to knock Antony down a peg.''

She glanced sideways at Nick, who still seemed
lost in thought. Placing a hand on his arm, she asked,
''You seem troubled. Are you all right?''

He turned and winked at her, all traces of his
gloomy mood vanishing. ''Of course. Just reminisc-
ing about childhood and fairy tales, I suppose.''

She leaned over and kissed him on the cheek, then
regretted being so forward. She kissed her brothers,
father and family friends in a similar manner all the
time without a second thought, whenever they needed
comfort or reassurance.

But kissing Nick, even innocently, was another
matter entirely. Because as he turned on the bench,
his handsome face moving within an inch of hers, she
realized kissing Nick could never be innocent.

Chapter Seven

A wave of panic swept through Isabella's stomach. Her hand still rested on Nick's arm, but before she could remove it he covered it with his own.

"Maybe we should head back to the palace," she whispered. But her rear failed to lift off the bench; her feet failed to move.

"Maybe we should."

But Nick didn't move, either. Their gazes locked, and Isabella realized they were alone on the street. Even the city noise, which had echoed up to them from below, faded into the back of her consciousness.

Nick's strong hands moved up to cradle her face, and he tilted his head past her baseball cap to bring his mouth down on hers. Gently at first, then more deeply. The restraint he'd shown during their storeroom encounter disappeared, replaced by open passion and hunger, as if her kiss provided him the sustenance needed to endure a long and desperate battle against an unseen enemy.

She shuddered and closed her eyes, allowing the sensation of his lips against hers—and his strong hands moving down to caress her neck, her shoulders, her back—to overwhelm her. Despite their very public location and the taboos facing her as a modern-day princess, she felt no urge to pull away. Instead, impulse overrode her common sense, and she clutched at his black T-shirt, pulling him down with her until they were nearly prone on the bus stop bench.

It's the Chianti, her mind warned, though she'd only had two glasses, about what she allowed herself at most royal functions. *You would never do this if you were thinking straight—you know absolutely nothing about him. What dirt might the tabloids find?*

But she was doing it, and she wanted to do it, despite the risks.

As Nick's powerful arms surrounded her, protected her, and as he kissed her ear, her cheek, her chin, she knew in the very core of her soul that Nick Black was her knight in shining armor. Only he could save her from a life that, in the two weeks since she'd met him, she'd come to view as empty. Isolating.

And so very, very lonely.

Tonight, in just a few hours, Nick had given her a magical glimpse of the life normal women lived. Women who could date whomever they chose. Who could eat at any restaurant and who could come and go as they pleased. Women whose fathers didn't worry about tabloids or public relations advisers or cameras with telephoto lenses.

Cameras...

"Oh, no, Nick, Nick, this is bad—" She could

barely get the words out as a rush of adrenaline coursed through her body. He raised his head to meet her gaze, and the naked desire filling his eyes made her want him all the more. But not here, not now.

His voice sounded harsh, as if the sheer effort of speaking taxed him. "I—I'm sorry, Your Highness, I—"

She put a finger to his lips. "Don't call me that. Follow me."

She pushed against his chest and maneuvered out from under him, flying off the bench and running toward the bakery with her head down. She glanced back, waving for him to follow her across the street. His forehead wrinkled in confusion, but he fished his backpack off the bench and did as she asked. Her hands shook as she knelt and inserted the key into the bottom of the heavy metal gate, then lifted it over her head so she could open the store's glass door. He remained silent, but once they were in the shop, with the gate safely closed behind them, he put a hand on her shoulder, turning her to face him.

"Please, Princess, I apologize. I should never have taken such a liberty—"

She cut him off with a shake of her head. "It's all right, really," she whispered, hoping he was reassured, though she could barely see his expression in the darkened shop. "We just had to get away from the palace fence. My father has dozens of security cameras mounted up there. The cameras on this side of the rose garden aren't turned on all the time, and I don't think they'd recognize me, especially when I'm wearing this cap and these horrible glasses, but—"

His fingers flexed on her shoulder, and the muscles of his face relaxed as he let out an audible breath. "So—so you're saying you're fine with—"

"Oh, yes. Absolutely." She reached up and forked her fingers into his dark hair, just behind his ears, as she'd dreamed of doing the day he'd knelt in front of her to study the medieval sword in the keep.

At his confused look, she stretched onto her tiptoes, pulled his face down to hers, and kissed him as she'd never kissed a man in her life.

At once Nick's arms came around her back, crushing her body against his larger one, and she tilted her head so he could kiss her more deeply, taking from him until her lower lip shook with need and her heart threatened to spasm in her chest.

Oh, yes. This was what she'd denied herself for so many years. And this one night, at least, she'd do her best to make up for lost time.

Still locked lip-to-lip, Nick eased her toward the back room of the bakery, where the smells of bagged flour and spices of every description mingled in her nostrils with the delicious, masculine scent she'd come to associate with Nick. She heard a thud as his backpack dropped to the floor, then he lowered her down, gently, until she felt cool tile beneath her and the soft give of an oversized flour sack where it leaned upright against the wall behind her. Still, Nick's insistent mouth never left hers, as if he feared she'd disappear if he allowed himself to break their intimate contact for even a second. She coaxed him down with her, easing his jean-clad hips against hers, untucking the back of his shirt and slipping her fingers underneath to caress his warm skin, then enjoying the rhythm of his body as it moved above her own.

"You have no idea how much I've wanted you," he moaned against her mouth.

She tried not to grin as he pushed against her, clearly needing to be unfettered from his jeans. "Oh, I think I know."

What would it be like to feel him inside her? Would it be every bit as rapturous as she dreamed? Every bit as freeing?

Or would it overwhelm her completely?

He pulled back, removed her glasses, and in one smooth move, he slid her baseball cap off her head and unwrapped the elastic holding her ponytail, allowing her hair to fall down her shoulders. "No need for these anymore. I need to see you, Princess."

Before he could move his mouth back to hers, she reached for his waistband and yanked the front of his black T-shirt free of his jeans. With bravado she hoped she wouldn't regret in the morning, she said, "Then I need to see you, too."

Within seconds, she had it over his head and tossed it behind him. When she looked up at him to gauge his reaction, she tried not to gasp in surprise. His bare shoulders seemed broader, his upper body more thickly muscled than she'd anticipated. A dusting of fine, dark hair covered his chest, and she couldn't stop herself from reaching out to run her fingers along his rib cage, up through the soft hair, then across to his shoulders. Every inch felt warm and silky and solid and wonderful. She began to move her fingers toward his back when she hit a small ridge, then another.

Scar after scar extended across the front and top of

his left shoulder, marring his beautifully smooth skin. The edges were rough, jagged, as if his skin had been torn and stitched hastily—or not at all. She squinted, trying to see more detail than the darkened room would allow. "This must have hurt terribly," she murmured, thinking of his scarred hand on that same side. Like those on his shoulder, the marks on his hand were raised and uneven. "Were you in a car accident?"

"No." He kissed her forehead and covered her hand with one of his, gently removing her fingers from his shoulder.

"Then what happened to you?" she whispered, her questioning eyes meeting his unfathomable ones. The mere thought he'd experienced such pain tore at her heart. "These were never treated by a doctor."

"It's a long story."

"A long story, or a secret?" She'd known even before they met that he had his secrets, but she hadn't imagined they'd be physical. Could the scars have something to do with why he shunned the public? Kept himself locked in his modern Boston office, protected by a dutiful secretary trained to turn away the world?

He squeezed her hand, then interlaced his fingers with hers. "A long story. And believe me, I want with all my heart to tell you. But now is not the time." He reached down to the bottom of her sweater, then pulled it over her head with the same passion she'd exhibited a moment before. His dark gaze bored into her, breaking down her last defenses even as one lean finger traced the lace along the top of her pink bra. "Wouldn't you agree?"

Without hesitating, she leaned forward and kissed his shoulder, willing the angry scars to heal. Willing *him* to heal. But despite spending most of her waking hours fighting to save the world's homeless, diseased and poor, she sensed saving Nick Black would be her most difficult challenge yet.

Nick jerked, and for a split second, she wondered if she'd done the wrong thing.

"Quick!" Nick grabbed Isabella's sweater and stuffed it into her hands. "Did you hear that?"

She didn't hear a thing, but the look on Nick's face scared her enough to yank the lilac sweater over her head anyway. "Hear what?"

Nick spun on his knees, retrieving his T-shirt from where it had landed on the side of a giant mixer. "C'mon." He popped his head and arms through the shirt then grabbed her hands, pulling her up and shoving her behind a large butcher-block-topped island. Then she heard it.

Laughter. *Stefano's* laughter. Horror froze her in place as she crouched behind the island. Nick pulled her hard against him, his thickly muscled arm squeezing her body to his so she couldn't be seen.

Within seconds, she heard the creak of the passageway door. Light from the tunnel illuminated a thin strip along the floor of the shop, then clicked off. She strained to see, but could only glimpse the hard tile and a few of the low cabinets without giving herself away.

Isabella's soon-to-be sister-in-law's voice reverberated through the tiny room. "Stefano, your father trusts my judgment. If he knew I not only allowed you to take off from the reception without telling him, but that I actually accompanied you—''

''Enough already, Amanda. The reception was nearly over when I left, and Antony had it covered. No one will notice.''

''Isabella will. As she should.''

''Isabella wasn't there.''

Amanda stopped walking, her high-heeled shoes visible beside the island, only inches from Nick and Isabella's hiding place.

''Are you certain? She didn't come on the hospital visit with me tonight. I assumed it was because she attended the reception with you.''

Stefano's feet came into view, just next to Amanda's, and Isabella swallowed hard. ''Nerina said she was scheduled elsewhere. Doing what, I don't know, but I don't care.''

They stopped talking, but their feet didn't move. Then something thunked against the island.

''Stef—'' Amanda's protest stopped, and Isabella realized Stef had stopped her argument with a kiss. Right on the other side of the island.

No, no, no! Isabella's mind screamed. What if things didn't stop at a kiss? She couldn't possibly allow it to continue without making her presence known, and then what?

Isabella glanced sideways at Nick, who didn't seem to share her concern. In fact, he could barely contain his laughter. He shook with the effort of keeping silent, and she shot him a venom-filled look.

He only shook harder.

Fortunately, just as Isabella decided she should stand up and announce herself, she heard a creak on the other side of the island, followed by footfalls as Stefano and Amanda continued walking toward the front door of the shop. Nick elbowed her, and Isabella turned to frown at him.

"The key," he hissed, then directed his gaze toward the front room. "They can't get out."

Isabella's mouth dropped open. She'd been so distracted when she and Nick entered the shop, she hadn't returned it to the top of the door frame. She upturned her empty palms to Nick, then felt the tiny pockets on the front of her capris while he patted his own pockets. No luck.

"It's supposed to be up here," Isabella heard Stefano telling Amanda in the front room. "The Alessandros wouldn't have moved it."

"Well, when did you last use it? And don't tell me you haven't used it since we met. I saw your hiking boots in the back of your Range Rover last week, and they were caked with mud."

Stef's laughter followed Amanda's teasing comment. "Okay, you caught me. But I distinctly remember returning the key. I'm always careful in case I want to take you out, you know."

Beside her, Isabella felt Nick shift. He darted out from behind the island, moving quickly but quietly. Panic rising in her throat as Stef and Amanda continued to tease each other, Isabella leaned out far enough to watch as he crossed to the flour sacks and grabbed his backpack and her ball cap and glasses, which they'd carelessly left behind when they'd rushed to hide. On the floor where the backpack had been she spied the shiny key, and gestured wildly until Nick saw her. He followed her pointing finger, grabbed the key, then tiptoed back to the island and placed it in her palm.

"Now what?" she mouthed.

He shrugged, his eyes wide.

She dropped her head against the island as quietly as possible. How could she have gotten herself into this mess?

"Hold on," Stefano's voice boomed from the front of the store. "You keep searching out here. I have one more place I can check."

Within seconds, Stefano was back in the room with them. He stood still for a second, then leaned on the island directly in front of them.

"Issy?" His voice came out so low she almost didn't hear him. "Come on out, Sis. I heard noise in here before we came in. And you're the only one who didn't come to tonight's reception."

She looked at Nick. His jerked his head toward the island and moved his mouth as if to say, *go ahead.*

She stood. Better that than having Stefano come around the island to see both of them hiding there.

Stefano's smug grin greeted her as she placed the key in his hand. He leaned forward, kissed her on the cheek, then whispered in her ear, "You're not as good at this as I am. Tell me next time you want to sneak out and I'll give you some pointers."

She considered punching him, just to wipe the mocking look off his face, but knew Amanda would hear.

Stef met her gaze, winked, then yelled to Amanda, "Found it!" With a final smirk, he spun on his heel and headed to the front of the store.

As soon as the metal gate closed behind Amanda

and Stefano, Nick collapsed against the island, holding his sides and laughing.

"You think that was funny?"

Nick snorted. Actually *snorted,* he laughed so hard. "Funniest thing I've seen in a long, long time. Think about it, Princess. Two world-famous royals sneaking around the back room of a hole-in-the-wall Italian bakery in the middle of the night just so they can get a little—"

"Get a little *what?*"

He cleared his throat and pretended to be serious. "A little…fresh air."

Isabella gave him a chastising shake of her head, but couldn't suppress a smile. "Okay, so it was funny. And I'm happy for Stef that he found someone levelheaded who loves him as much as Amanda does."

"They are in love. No doubt about that."

"But what if Stef had caught us outside? Or worse, what if a reporter had seen us? Or even a tourist with a camera? We should never have done this."

Nick pushed himself up from the tile floor. This time, his serious expression wasn't for show. "Do you really mean that?"

"Yes. No. I don't know. I—"

He moved closer, then put a hand on her shoulder. She loved the reassurance his touch gave her, but right now it didn't seem to calm her.

"You needed to get out and experience some freedom," he said. "And to see that it's okay for you to be with a man without worrying about what the tabloids might say."

"I see men all the time."

"But not alone. Not since you went to Harvard." He lifted his hand from her shoulder to cup her chin, forcing her to meet his gaze. "I understand why, but it doesn't have to be that way. Life's too short for you to remain a cooped-up virgin."

Anger mingled with embarrassment in her gut. "I never said—"

"No shame in it, Princess. And before you ask, no, the whole world doesn't know. Just supposition on my part." He ran his thumb along her cheek and studied her for a moment, as if deciding how best to phrase what he wanted to say. "Trust me when I say I've seen too many women waste their entire lives waiting for the time to be 'safe' to follow their hearts. While your circumstance is unique, I couldn't stand to see that happen to you. You're too special a person. You deserve some happiness." He shot a pointed look toward the front of the store. "Like your brother and Amanda."

"Maybe," she whispered. "But what about my family? You should have seen what my father went through with Stefano before he met Amanda. Out gambling at all hours, refusing to attend palace events…and it's different with a daughter. Look at what the Grimaldis have endured with Princess Stefanie. She even lived with a traveling circus, just because a man—"

He shushed her with a look. "You're not your brother, and you're certainly not Princess Stefanie. You're Isabella diTalora. And your judgment is sound. You want to go on a date, not join a traveling circus. And no one, not even the tabloids, will fault you or your family for that. You have to believe that.

And any man who is lucky enough to date you will believe it, too.''

''Nick—''

''Just think about it. Tonight doesn't have to be a one-time event for you. If you want to see men, then see them. I'm sure there are dozens of men who would kill for the opportunity to take you out, even once. Wear the glasses and hat if you want, but soon you'll realize you don't need them.''

She must have looked as doubtful as she felt, because he whispered, ''Just promise me you'll think about it. Take a risk and live your life. Find someone to love. You'll regret it if you don't.''

A tear rolled down her cheek before she could stop it. Had anyone ever spoken to her as he did? Her family cared about her, but no one ever bothered to ask if she was happy. They assumed it because that's what she'd allowed them to see. And she had to admit, even if they had asked, she'd have told them she was perfectly happy, thank you very much. Only Nick perceived the truth.

She touched the smooth cotton of his black T-shirt, drawing from his strength, then letting the pads of her fingers linger on his firm shoulder. She could detect his raised scars, even through the fabric. As magical as their night was, he gave her the impression he wanted her to date other men. What could have damaged him so profoundly that he felt he could not love? Why couldn't he take the same risk he encouraged her to take?

She took a deep breath, forcing herself to keep her tears in check. ''Okay, I promise. I'll think about it.''

''Good.''

She looked him in the eye, but left her fingers on his shoulder. "Tell me, though, what do *you* need, Nick? You keep yourself even more isolated than I do. You see no one. Not in public, not in private. Perhaps that's why you understand me so well. Because you're in need, too?"

His eyes narrowed, and she knew he erected fortifications around his heart she might never penetrate. But she had to try, at least one more time.

"I can't tell you why, Princess. I want to, but—" He leaned forward, putting his forehead against hers. "I know it sounds like I'm trying to evade your questions. I'm not. I really do want to tell you, more than I've ever wanted to tell anyone. But it's very complicated."

"More complicated than my life? You can't possibly fear the paparazzi or bad press as much as I do."

"You have no idea."

Nick removed her hand from his scarred shoulder for the second time that night. He hated to put her off, knowing that if anyone on earth might believe his story, it would be Princess Isabella.

But experience told him he needed to protect himself, and to protect her. If she heard his story and decided to stick by him, as Coletta had, he couldn't live with himself.

And though the tabloids might not skewer her for going on a simple date with an ordinary man, they'd rip her to shreds if she chose to date a man who claimed to be immortal. Her family would be hurt, she'd be convinced she was right to keep herself isolated and she'd be even worse off than before.

"Listen, Princess," he guided her away from the butcher block island, toward the passage, "it's late, and we should both get some sleep. I have to get that report to you first thing in the morning, and you're going to need to prepare for your meeting with the museum board."

The corners of her mouth tipped up, but he could still see pain in her eyes at his inability to share his secrets. "All right," she replied. "But you aren't off the hook."

"I didn't think so."

They strolled through the passage and into the storeroom hand in hand, without speaking. As they climbed the worn stone steps leading from the storeroom to the main area of the keep, they let go, drifting to opposite sides of the hallway. Entering the palace together, yet feeling the need once again to maintain a professional distance.

When they reached the door to his guest suite, Isabella broke the silence. "Thank you, Nick. Dinner was wonderful." She turned to face him in the semidarkness. "It was a wonderful birthday gift, and I won't forget it."

"Nor I. Happy twenty-ninth." Sensing more was needed, despite the fact they were in a public hall and anyone could happen along, he leaned over and kissed her cheek. He breathed in the sweet, fresh scent of her hair, and nearly lost his resolve. Forcing himself to pull back, he added, "I'll deliver the report to Nerina first thing."

He saw her swallow. "Thank you."

He turned the knob, and was halfway into the room

when a thought occurred to him. Stepping back into the hall, he called to Isabella's back, "Princess?"

She froze, then spun around, anticipation on her face.

"I've been thinking about your offer to fly Anne over here. I do think I'll take you up on it."

The look of anticipation vanished, replaced by what he'd come to recognize as her "professional" expression.

"Of course. I'll arrange to have a ticket delivered to her in Boston at your convenience and will have the staff prepare a guest suite for her." She gave him a curt nod, making it clear she didn't care to talk any more that night. "If you need anything else, just let Nerina know. Good night."

"Good night," he answered, but she was already halfway down the hall. He closed the door to his room, then pounded the wall with his fist hard enough to cause bruising by morning, though it was his heart that would likely ache.

He hated to hurt Isabella. He didn't regret taking her out and proving to her that she could enjoy life, but he should have resisted her kisses.

He leaned his head against the cool stone wall and mimicked his favorite *Star Trek* line, "Resistance is futile." Isabella diTalora fit too perfectly into his arms. He had no more strength to resist her than a starving man would if offered a gourmet feast.

Without thinking, his fingers drifted to the scars on his shoulder, obtained in battle two years before he'd met Rufina. Nearly all the knights he knew suffered injuries at one time or another, either on the battlefield or during training, and their bodies bore the scars. His own wounds healed as well as could be hoped back in the twelfth century, without the benefit of modern medicine, and he hadn't thought much about them since.

But Isabella did. She cared, just as she cared about his isolation and realized that he didn't live this way by choice.

He turned his head enough to look out the modern window that now occupied one wall of his small suite. Below, elegant roses and clipped boxwood hedges filled the area that once held King Bernardo's herb garden and a well. To his left, the main area of the palace, which hadn't even existed during his years here, stretched out across its majestic hilltop perch, overlooking the casinos, theaters and business district below. A lone bright light shone in the area occupied by the family's private apartments, but otherwise, all were dimmed for the evening.

He couldn't help but wonder if the light belonged to Isabella. And if their night on the town left her as agitated and full of need as it left him. They belonged together, body and soul, and he sensed she felt the same way. Or she would, if they spent more time alone.

But he couldn't have her, not until he broke the curse, *if* he could even break the curse. She deserved to see someone else, and he had to let her. Just as he should have let Coletta go, no matter how much he'd wanted her to remain with him.

He sighed as the bright light in the main palace was extinguished. At least with Anne around to help with the museum project, more of his time could be freed up to follow his own quest.

He closed his eyes, praying that he might finally break the curse. Never had he felt so close, nor had he ever felt more desperate.

And in the meantime, having his secretary present in the storeroom would keep him from succumbing to temptation where Princess Isabella was concerned.

If he kissed her again, they'd both be lost.

Chapter Eight

Isabella nodded to the familiar night guard stationed outside her palace apartments, then opened the main door and flipped on the light. As she expected, the staff had completed their usual whirlwind preparations for the next day. A typewritten copy of her schedule sat perfectly centered on the small cherry writing desk beside her door, courtesy of Nerina. A chocolate-colored silk suit appropriate for her morning appointments hung on a small rack beside her armoire, with matching shoes and a prepacked purse neatly laid out on a chair nearby. A black pantsuit of lightweight wool hung behind the silk, with a small note attached indicating it would be appropriate for her meeting with the museum staff and the dinner she'd planned with her father, should she choose to change.

The brocade comforter topping her bed was neatly folded back, leaving her Egyptian cotton sheets exposed. A deeply cut crystal pitcher containing cool water rested on her nightstand beside a matching tumbler, and she knew a freshly fluffed bathrobe awaited her inside the luxurious marble bathroom.

Here, nothing had changed. Inside her, everything changed.

Part of her wanted to return to Nick's room, to knock on his door and to kiss him again the second he opened it. Before he could think, before he could make an excuse or put her off. Every molecule in her body screamed for his touch, and the same overwhelming need tortured him, she knew it did. She might be a virgin and fairly inexperienced with men, but she hadn't just fallen off the turnip truck, either. No one could mistake the hunger in Nick's kisses, the need in his gaze or the admiring way his hands caressed her body.

So what held him back?

She kicked off her flats beside the front door, still amazed she'd ventured out in public dressed in such casual clothes, then picked up her schedule from the desk.

Beneath the schedule, a sheet of ivory stationery bearing Federico's neat handwriting caught her attention. Instantly, her hand went to her stomach. The boys! She'd promised to tuck them in, and in her excitement at going out on the town, she'd completely forgotten. Federico had to be furious, and the boys so disappointed. How could she have been so thoughtless?

She picked up the page and began reading Federico's always-formal Italian.

Dearest Sister,

Arturo and Paolo were naturally saddened that you were unable to read to them this evening. Whether your absence was accidental or intentional, please accept my deepest gratitude. I enjoyed having the opportunity to spend some quiet hours with my sons, and for the first time in a long while, we read and sang songs and truly enjoyed ourselves. I needed to see for myself that I can be comfortable laughing again, and wouldn't have done so without being pushed into spending some time alone with the children.

After the boys went to sleep, I phoned Nerina and enquired as to your whereabouts. She said little save that you had a prior engagement. I then realized, dear sister, that today is your birthday. Please forgive me for failing to give you my heartfelt good wishes. I do hope you found your own enjoyment tonight—you deserve some happiness after all you have done for Arturo, Paolo and me since Lucrezia's death. Indeed, for all you have done for our family. Until tonight, when you were not here, I failed to realize the many sacrifices you make for us.

Again, please accept my apologies, and my gratitude for all you do. If you wish, Arturo and Paolo would be happy to share a birthday cake with you tomorrow evening. But if you have other plans, I encourage you to pursue them.

Ever in your debt,
Federico

Isabella blinked in disbelief, then read the note again. Gratitude for *missing* the boys' bedtime story.

Not what she'd expected, yet she didn't doubt Federico's sincerity.

She scribbled a note on her schedule reminding her to stop by Federico's apartments the next night. Then, smiling to herself, she folded Federico's letter for safekeeping in her nightstand. Someday Federico might learn not to be so formal, at least with his own siblings, but for now, she'd treasure his heartfelt words.

She slid the nightstand drawer closed, thinking that perhaps Nick was right after all. Perhaps her family would understand if she dipped her toe in the relationship waters. Not that she'd allow herself to get caught kissing a man on a public bench—that had been a dreadful lapse in judgment—but what harm could there possibly be in sharing a candlelight dinner under the stars, enjoying good conversation and a glass of wine, provided her date didn't mind a flashbulb going off now and then?

Unless, of course, the man with whom she shared that dinner harbored a secret the tabloids could expose, then use to destroy her family's reputation.

She sat on the edge of her bed and propped her chin in her hands. Nick had taken pains to evade the paparazzi's cameras at the airport the day he'd arrived in San Rimini. And tonight she'd been well-disguised, so his chances of being photographed were minimal. Still, she'd sensed he remained on edge, constantly alert for anyone who might snap a photo of them. But was his edginess because he feared for her, or for himself as well?

And why did he seem to be encouraging her to see

other men? Did he genuinely believe a relationship between the two of them was impossible, despite the undeniable chemistry they shared? What secret could be so devastating?

She threaded her fingers through her hair. "Why, Nick? Why won't you tell me?"

Pushing off the bed, she slid into feet into her flats and strode out the front door. The guard jumped when she stopped beside him.

"Your Serene Highness!"

"Sorry to disturb you. I was wondering, do you know what time Jack Donnington arrives in the morning?"

"Your father's chief of security? I believe he is here now. He was briefing the night watch at your brother Antony's apartments when I came on duty, Your Highness. If you need to speak with him, you might try ringing his office." In the dim light of the hallway, she could see the guard's brow pucker in concern. "I—I hope you have not been dissatisfied with my service?"

"No." She smiled at him in reassurance. "You've always done a fabulous job. There's simply an issue I was hoping Mr. Donnington might investigate for me."

Relieved, the guard gushed his thanks, then wished her good-night.

Within minutes, Isabella had the security chief on her private line. She quickly explained her needs, then asked for his discretion. "This is only for my own information, Jack. I don't wish for you to take any action, regardless of what you find. And I also ask that you do not speak to my father about this request."

"As you wish, Your Highness," the former British MI6 agent replied. "I'll get right on it."

"Thank you. But please, only pursue it if you're not otherwise occupied with my father's needs. This is a low priority."

"Understood."

She replaced the receiver, satisfied that she'd soon have her answer—or at least a hint. Part of her knew Nick would be disappointed in her going behind his back, but at the same time, as his employer, she had a right to double-check his background. "It can't be that bad," she tried to convince herself. She knew from her prior background check that he didn't have a criminal record. No arrests, no contact with the police at all. No one as kind and caring as Nick Black could have any sizeable skeletons in his closet, could he?

No matter what, she had to know. It was the only way she'd know which approach to take to try to convince him she wouldn't think worse of him. And that he could love her without fear. Because tonight, under the moonlight and stars of San Rimini, she'd fallen in love with Nick Black. And she wanted nothing more than for him to fall in love with her.

The glowing red numbers on her bedside clock flipped to 1:00 a.m., and she realized her birthday had ended. Twenty-eight was a memory. And next year she'd be...

She let out a groan. *Thirty.*

Where had her twenties gone? Tomorrow, she'd be back to her usual routine, hopping from one event to another with little time for herself. Two weeks ago it wouldn't have bothered her. Tonight, however, it weighed on her heavily.

She walked out of her apartments past the guard again, who by this time probably wondered about her state of mind, and turned toward the keep. Nick would be long asleep—at least, she hoped he would be—but she deserved one more birthday gift.

Anne Jones flipped through the notebook on Nick's desk, carefully comparing his handwritten notes to those she'd typed. Over her shoulder, she remarked, "I'm quite impressed, sir. You've accomplished a great deal in only a few weeks. The museum board must have been quite satisfied with your progress."

Nick grunted a response as he dragged a large crate out of the stall he'd started cataloguing a few days before. Since discovering the scroll with his name on it, precious little else had come to light. Not even the fairy-tale book. He could have sworn he'd left it behind in the stall when he took Isabella out to dinner, but now, three days later, he still hadn't located it.

Once he maneuvered the crate into an open area for unpacking, he went in search of the crowbar so he could pry off the top. He'd been so distracted by the princess, and by their passionate encounter in the bakery, that he'd completely forgotten what she'd said about *The Cursed Knight*. As soon as she'd told him the story that night on the bus stop bench, he'd intended to check the book and see if it contained the tale.

Of course, getting his shirt whipped off by a woman for the first time in, how long?—he did a quick computation in his head and decided it had been at least thirty years, since he'd lived in Dallas, under another alias—well, that tended to distract a guy from tearing into a fairy-tale book, even if it might hold the key to his curse.

But once morning rolled around, and he'd started preparing his report for the museum board, his mind focused once again on the reason he'd come to San Rimini in the first place. He'd raced to the stall, expecting the book to be in plain sight, but no luck. Now, after three full days of searching, he had to conclude that sometime during the night, Isabella had changed her mind and decided to keep it.

"Rotten timing," he muttered aloud. He couldn't exactly ask her to give it back now. Or just show up at her apartments and ask to take a look-see. But he had to know about the tale. In centuries of searching, he'd never found a more solid lead. His entire existence—or at least the *length* of his existence—could depend on it.

"Sir?" Anne looked up from the desk in alarm. "Something I can help you with?"

"No. Just talking to myself." He sucked in a deep breath, then let it out slowly, slowly. Being around so many medieval San Riminian artifacts, far more than he'd acquired in years of collecting in Boston, and seeing his own name tucked in the midst of those artifacts gave him an edge of desperation. He hadn't been himself lately, and he needed to get a grip so he wouldn't miss something critical during his search.

Come to think of it—he glanced across the room at his secretary—Anne hadn't seemed herself since she'd arrived in San Rimini, either. In Boston, she'd always been calm, reserved, efficient. But here, the castle walls seemed to disturb her. She jumped at the slightest sound, and more than once, he'd caught her staring at the contents of the storeroom as if the place held ghosts instead of stacks of crates.

He couldn't blame her for being jittery, though. His office boasted floor-to-ceiling windows, a high-tech ventilation system, easy access to several delis and a view of Post Office Square, where Anne could enjoy her lunch in the sunshine.

And intentionally modern décor to keep him from focusing on all he'd lost in the past.

Here, they were surrounded with paintings of long-dead monarchs, the smell of rotting fabrics and the occasional sculpted marble head. Instead of a desk with a panoramic view of Boston's Financial District, Anne stared at a gray stone wall. And running out to a deli was out of the question, unless she wanted to go through security checks at the palace door and again at the front gate.

He located the crowbar and set it on top of the crate. ''Tell you what, Anne. You've been down here for hours. I'd like your help on a different project, if you don't mind spending time in the palace library.''

She spun in the chair, obviously anxious to leave the storeroom. ''Yes?''

''Look through the royal family's collection of books and on the Internet for me, and see if you can find anything on an old San Riminian fairy tale. It's called *The Cursed Knight,* or something similar.''

Her eyes widened and he thought a look of trepidation passed over her face, but it disappeared before he could be sure. ''Did you say *The Cursed Knight?*''

"Yes. Are you familiar with it?"

She shook her head. "No. I, ah, I haven't heard of that one. But I'm not the expert you are." She set her pen down on the desk, rolling it around with her finger as she spoke. "I—I thought you were interested in artifacts, sir. I wasn't expecting to do literary research. I don't believe you've had me do anything like it before."

"I'm taking a new tack with my research."

She frowned and opened her mouth as if about to say something, but apparently thought better of it. Gathering up her purse and notebook, she merely said, "Well, I'll endeavor to find it."

"Thanks."

She dusted off the front of her black skirt and smoothed her graying red hair into place, then, straightening her back as if she might meet the king himself in the hallway, she took the stairs toward the main palace.

As soon as she left, Nick returned to the crate and pried off the lid. Weird. Anne never questioned him before. He'd underestimated the strength of her preference for modern Boston over the back rooms of San Rimini's historic buildings. He'd have to give her a raise when they returned home.

Even as the thought occurred to him, he cursed himself for it. He couldn't go home again. Not permanently, anyway. If he failed in his search this time, he'd need to assume a new identity and start over. Too many people would have heard of him as a result of the museum project, Anne might start to ask questions, and besides, the Bloody Mary episode taught him the importance of maintaining his fifteen-to-twenty year rule.

Tossing the crate lid aside with more fervor than necessary, he swore aloud. He couldn't fail. Just couldn't. Too many more years of this half-alive, half-dead existence and he'd end up in a loony bin for sure. Besides, where would he go next? It had to be somewhere he could disappear in a crowd, somewhere without modern computers keeping track of the population and without constant requests for identification. Unfortunately, modern technology had revolutionized the world during the past twenty years; at this pace, he'd have nowhere left to hide in another twenty.

Besides the risk of getting caught, if he let himself think about it for more than a minute, he knew he'd realize how much he suddenly had to live for. The thought of losing Isabella, even though he didn't exactly *have* her, tore at his gut.

He swept aside mounds of shredded packing material until his hands hit something solid. Wrapping his fingers around the item, he pulled gently, realizing at once he'd located another book.

Come on, fairy tales, he wished as he cracked open the cover.

Iudicium, the faded word on the first page read. Judgment. Then below that, *Maleficarum.* Witches. Witch trials.

A bolt of pain slashed him from temple to temple, along the same pathway his headaches traveled. He flipped a few more pages, trying to ignore the hammering in his head even as his mind filled with the horrible images described in the text. Burning at the stake. Torture. Forced confessions. Long-term imprisonment. And every single instance documented in the book took place in southern Europe during the centuries surrounding his birth.

It could mean nothing. Or it could mean everything. Forcing himself to settle, he carried the book to the desk and cautiously began to turn the pages, scouring each account for anything that might give him a clue to Rufina.

Seventy-six pages of horrors later, his chest threatened to collapse inward. After reading accounts of trials in Germany, Genoa and Spain, he came across a section that couldn't be ignored—seventeen women tried for witchcraft in San Rimini over a frenzied six-month period in 1199.

Only nine years after he'd been cursed.

Vision blurring with the pain of his headache, he scanned the descriptions of the accused—their hair, their ages, their occupations—alert for any detail that might clue him in to Rufina's whereabouts, if she'd been tried and released.

"Sir?" Nick flinched as footsteps approached from behind. "Sorry to disturb you, sir, but I found what you needed."

"Already?" He slammed the book closed before looking up at Anne.

She glanced down at the book in his hands, then returned her focus to him and shrugged. "It was quite easy, sir. I did an Internet search using the terms 'cursed knight' and 'San Rimini' and found a few sites that mentioned it. Looks to be an older tale, not commonly told. And apparently unique to the area of

San Rimini and Venice. Here." She held out a sheaf of papers. "I printed out the relevant information."

He swallowed and accepted the papers, though he wasn't sure he had the stamina to absorb all the information suddenly flying at him. "Thank you, Anne. Um, I know it's early, but why don't you take a break? Go for a walk, see the city."

She eyed him curiously. "Are you certain, sir? I don't mind—"

He waved her off. "Go. You deserve some fresh air." And he needed the privacy.

"All right." She glanced again at the book, and at the papers she'd printed off for him. "But if you think you're on to something important, I'm more than happy to pursue—"

"Go!" The command came out more forcefully than he'd have liked, but his head pounded with the force of a cannon. He closed his eyes, opened them to give her an apologetic look. "Sorry. That was uncalled for. I'm a bit worn out, I suppose."

"Why don't I come back in a couple hours? Just to check in?" She shot a pointed look at the nearly empty bottle of aspirin on the desktop. "If I pass by a pharmacy, I'll grab you some more."

"You know which brand I prefer. Thank you, Anne. You're a lifesaver."

As soon as the sound of her footsteps disappeared, he shuffled through the printouts she'd given him. The so-called fairy tale told his story, no doubt. And he had to credit Princess Isabella with a good memory. The tale played out, in all its versions, exactly as she'd told him. Cursed with immortality, the knight became an outcast, never welcomed in any home from that day forward.

And never breaking his curse. In any variation of the story.

"So much for your nanny's version," Nick grumbled, shoving the papers to the side of the desk. Perhaps later he'd have Anne check further, but he doubted he'd find his answers. Instead, he popped the white top of the clear plastic aspirin bottle, fished out the last three white pills, then swallowed them dry.

Ignoring the bitter taste in his mouth, he reopened the book on witch trials, trying not to envision the agony of the poor women who'd been dragged from their homes and accused of witchcraft for one reason or another. Thank goodness the human race had evolved during his lifetime.

He flipped a few more pages, scanning description after agonizing description, until his gaze fell on a passage that took his breath away.

The book described a proceeding involving a red-haired woman of approximately five and forty years, arrested in the San Riminian borderlands, accused of using the Devil to aid her in healing local farmers. A young man claimed the red-haired woman, whose name was not given, had been called to heal his father's headaches, but instead put his father under a spell causing the older man to become paralyzed on one side of his body. After being visited by the accused, witnesses claimed the old man drooled endlessly, which could only be caused by the Devil inhabiting his body.

Rufina had been a healer, he remembered. And he assumed the old man had suffered a stroke, since in medieval times many believed strokes to be a partial paralysis that resulted after one had been touched by the Devil. The so-called witch denied the charges, and brought several witnesses to testify on her behalf, including her grown son, who was described as a farmer from a nearby village who walked with a limp.

Nick rubbed a thumb over the ache in his head. This had to be his Rufina. If she'd been forty-five years old in 1199, that would have made her thirty-six when she'd met him. And she'd told him her son was fourteen. Sounded right to him.

He scanned the rest of the discussion, skipping over the sections on the woman's torture until he came to the end of the passage. His heart clenched as he read the woman's verdict. The panel of church officials hearing Rufina's case deemed her to be a witch and a heretic.

He knew she was a witch, or whatever one might term a person who possessed powers he couldn't understand. But they couldn't have found her guilty. *They couldn't!* She didn't deserve it. And he didn't deserve it.

No, no, no! The room swam before Nick's eyes. His head thrummed and a choked cry escaped him as he zeroed in on the final line of text.

The witch had been put to death immediately, in the main square of the local village, by burning.

Chapter Nine

Isabella gave her oldest brother, Prince Antony, a quick kiss on the cheek and wished him good luck in his business meeting with the German foreign minister before ducking into her own office. Their pre-meeting lunch, attended by the entire royal family and a fleet of reporters, crackled with tension. Despite her usual interest in San Rimini's foreign affairs, she'd had a difficult time concentrating on the discussion.

Halfway through the salad course, Nerina pressed a note into Isabella's hand saying that Mr. Donnington needed to speak with her as soon as possible, that he had important information to share.

Over fresh tilapia fillets and wild rice, Isabella couldn't help but turn the possibilities over in her mind. Could Nick have been involved in some financial scandal, or worse, a sexual scandal at his last job? Surely her initial background check would have found something of that magnitude.

Maybe he was simply a divorcé, and therefore feared getting involved in another relationship. Perfectly understandable. But wait, could he still be married? Some Third World marriage, perhaps, that wouldn't have come to light during her cursory check, but that Jack Donnington would have discovered?

During dessert, she'd fiddled with her napkin under the table while the burly German across the table discussed the stability of the Euro, all the while wondering what Nick's secret could be and trying to put the worst possible spin on things in her mind so she'd be prepared for whatever her father's security chief might reveal. None of her terrible imaginings meshed with her beliefs about his basic personality, however. And certainly nothing she dreamed up explained his physical scars.

Once she'd closed the office door behind her, she rushed to her desk, and ignoring her e-mail and the flashing answering machine, she dialed the security chief's extension.

"Donnington."

"Yes, Mr. Donnington. This is Princess Isabella."

"Your Serene Highness." His tone was solemn, deferential. "I made some progress on my investigation. If you have a moment, I would like to meet with you in person to discuss my findings."

"Of course. I'm in my office now, if you're free."

"I shall come at once. And it might be best if we're alone, Your Highness."

"Understood."

She worried her lip with her teeth, calculating how long it would take the security chief to reach her office from his, which was outside her father's apartments. Whatever he'd found couldn't be good news, or he'd have told her on the phone. Thankfully for her bottom lip, he strode into her open office door within a few minutes, closing it behind him.

"Please," she urged him to make himself comfortable in a nearby chair, "no need for formality. I take it you've found something concrete?"

"You be the judge." He took the seat and held out a manila folder, which she accepted.

"These are your findings on Mr. Black?"

"Yes. Or more accurately, my lack of findings."

When she frowned, he explained, "In all my years of doing background checks, Your Highness, I've never come across anyone like him. While I found an American social security number and birth records easily enough, on further scrutiny, they didn't check out. The social security number was originally issued to a man who died in 1967, at the age of seventy-one. I looked for the individuals listed as his parents on Mr. Black's birth certificate, and so far as I can tell, they never existed. Made up. So I tried to confirm Mr. Black's birth with the actual hospital listed on his birth certificate, and they informed me that they weren't in existence until two years after Mr. Black's apparent date of birth. So he couldn't have possibly been born there. He has no tax records, no property records, no educational records that I could find. I could search further, but I doubt anything would come to light."

Isabella took the seat across from Mr. Donnington, crossing her legs at the ankles in the formal-but-interested-in-what-you-have-to-say pose she generally used with reporters, and tried to keep her face neutral, despite the fact her stomach suddenly wanted to give back her lunch. "What do you make of it all, Jack?"

The security chief let out a deep breath, apparently considering how best to phrase his conclusions. "This man has taken great pains not to exist on paper, Your Highness. Most of what I learned was only accessible by calling in favors from some of my old chums at MI6 and the CIA. To most of the world, he's invisible."

Isabella studied Jack's face, trying to absorb the information and further gauge his opinion. "Could he be a criminal? Someone running from the law?"

"I doubt it. Criminals aren't usually this good at covering their tracks. On the contrary, at first I believed he might be a former CIA spook. Or in the United States' Witness Protection Program. Someone whose identity had been wiped clean for a reason."

"But you don't believe that now? Why?"

"I checked with my contacts in the U.S. While they would never reveal the identity of anyone they're trying to cover, they did give me enough information to conclude that he isn't in Witness Protection. Or a former operative." He leaned forward, reaching for the manila folder. "May I?"

She handed it to him. "Of course."

"As I was checking other hospitals in New Jersey, near where he claimed to have been born, I found this quite by accident in Lakehurst. After I saw it, all theories went out the window." He handed her a black-and-white photograph about the size of her palm. "I simply cannot explain it."

Isabella stared down at the face in the photo, unable to speak.

"I was perplexed by it, too," Mr. Donnington admitted with a shrug. "The man in the photo went by a slightly different name. Dan Black. At first I thought it must be a relative, since I've never seen two people look more alike. I tried to trace him, figuring I could use him to learn more about Nick, but I hit the exact same wall. Inaccurate birth records, and in his case, no social security number. Soon after this photo was taken, he disappeared. There is no record of where he moved, and I couldn't locate a death certificate." The security chief took the photograph and carefully placed it back in the folder. "Your Highness, I know you do not wish for King Eduardo to know about this inquiry, and I have honored your request. But I believe your father should be involved. This could be a matter of national security."

Nick? While he had the intelligence, and the access, to pose a threat to the royal family, she'd had to wheel and deal to get him to leave the United States. *She'd* sought *him* out. If he'd wanted to harm the family, he'd already had ample opportunity.

Isabella shook her head. "No. I know what you've discovered is perplexing, but I don't believe he's here for any nefarious purposes. I'd appreciate handling this one myself."

"Your Highness, something triggered you to come to me. Something you felt wasn't right about the man. If you confront him with your findings, you could be putting yourself in grave danger. For all we know—"

She raised a hand, cutting him off. "For all we know, the man in this picture *is* a relative. And that relative might have had a reason to be protected, too."

He let out an exasperated sigh, the same one she'd heard him use whenever her father argued in favor of lightening up on palace security in order to make guests feel more welcome. "I'd feel better about it if you'd at least allow me to speak with Mr. Black first, Your Highness. He could be dangerous, and I have experience with these matters. I should be able to ferret out more information without raising any suspicions on his part."

"You've already gone above and beyond the call of duty, Jack. I'm amazed you were able to scout out so much information in only three days. But I assure you, I can handle it from here. If I need you for anything, anything at all, or feel my safety might be in jeopardy, I'll notify you immediately." She stood, making it clear her decision was final.

"If you promise, Your Highness. Please, be careful."

"I will." As Donnington opened the door, she added, "Could you do me a favor? On your way out, let Nerina know I'll be unable to meet my father for dinner tonight. I'll reschedule as soon as possible."

"Of course."

When she was once again alone in the office, she sat at her desk and studied the file, reading all the information page by page, then rereading it. None of it made sense. She pulled out the photograph so she could examine it more closely. The image of the man carrying a stretcher looked so much like Nick, yet it clearly wasn't him. Grabbing a magnifying glass from her desk drawer, she inspected the photograph in detail. Several raised scars criss-crossed the back of the man's left hand where he grasped one side of the hospital stretcher.

Isabella closed her eyes and let out a ragged breath. Nick definitely had secrets. Secrets bigger than she'd imagined over lunch. And despite Jack Donnington's warning, she knew now she had to get at the truth. The question was how.

She fingered the photo, wishing she could comfort Nick or at least help him in some way. It pained her that he had to carry his burden—whatever his burden might be—alone.

Isabella slid the magnifying glass back into the desk drawer along with the file, pocketed the photograph, then locked the drawer.

"Sir? I have a bottle of aspirin for you. I didn't see the brand you prefer, but I think these should work." Anne swept into the storeroom, handing Nick a small green bottle with an Italian label. He scanned it, though he wasn't really interested. At this point, not much could dull his pain. It traveled down from his head to affect every bone, muscle and pore in his body.

"Thanks, Anne. I'm sure it'll be fine. Oh, before you go for the day, could you do one more thing for me? I need the phone number for the antiquities department at the University of San Rimini."

"Of course." She took a step back, lingering by the doorway and watching as he withdrew his hanging files from the desk drawer. "What is wrong, sir, if you don't mind my asking? Is there some problem?"

Nick placed the hanging files on top of the stack of papers and reference books already filling a cardboard box perched on his desk chair, then met Anne's worried look with a half smile. "Not a problem, Anne. But for reasons I'd rather keep to myself for now, I've decided not to continue my position here with Princess Isabella. I'm going to call a professor I've consulted once or twice and see if he can recommend anyone else for the job. As soon as I have a replacement and can hand off my notes, I'd like to head back to Boston."

"I see," Anne murmured, though her face made it plain she didn't see.

"I'm sorry not to have told you," he apologized, knowing Anne would never question him if she wasn't deeply concerned. "I wanted to be sure I could find a suitable replacement first, since I don't want my departure to delay the museum expansion."

"Have you spoken with the princess about your decision?"

"No. But as soon as I speak with the professor, I will. I want the princess to realize…" *That it has nothing to do with her.*

Even though it had everything to do with her. He might discover some tidbit useful to his quest if he stayed in San Rimini, but given what he'd found already, that Rufina had been dead for almost as long as he'd been alive, the odds were slim to none. Centuries of sacrificing hadn't worked, so he had to assume that when Rufina died, the key to breaking the curse died with her.

And with every day he stayed, searching for an answer that likely didn't exist, he risked being exposed. He couldn't accept that risk any longer. Not for himself, not for Anne or Roger, who would certainly be questioned about his outrageous claim of immortality, and definitely not for Princess Isabella.

Just as bad, every day he stayed meant spending more time around the princess, knowing that he could never, ever have her. And knowing he'd have to distance himself to keep her from falling for him as hard as he'd fallen for her. He didn't know if he could take it, not after the way he'd lost Coletta.

"Realize?" Anne prodded.

He shrugged and dropped his microcassette recorder into the cardboard box. "That I'm not indispensable to the project, I suppose."

"The princess may argue with that. She did go to great lengths to hire you, as I'm sure you recall."

"Well, I'll do my best to give my successor the same resources I had. I might even recommend Roger for the job. He's certainly qualified."

Nick folded down the flaps on the box, interweaving them so the top wouldn't pop open. "It'll take me several days to get everything in order, Anne. In the meantime, you're free to see the city, since I won't need you down here. Gamble, sit on the beach, tour the museums. San Rimini is a beautiful country, at least once you get outside this frigid old room, so you should really take advantage." Not that he wanted to think about San Rimini's white sand beaches or its posh casinos, not if he couldn't share them with Isabella or enjoy a night like the one they'd spent at the outdoor café.

He forced a grin to his face, though it took Herculean effort. He needed to convince Anne nothing out of the ordinary had happened, that he'd simply made a business decision. "I'd also appreciate it if you could check on plane tickets and reserve something back to Boston early next week. Otherwise,'' he swept a hand in the general direction of the Strada il Teatro, ''your vacation awaits.''

She nodded slowly, as if processing the turn of events. ''All right, sir. I'll make the reservations today.''

''Ever the professional. Thank you.''

With that, she turned on her sensible heels and left. Nick moved the cardboard box to the desk and labeled it, trying to keep his mind focused on the task at hand. But when he glimpsed the worn medieval book on the corner of the desktop, and thought of the descriptions of suspected witches being burned alive, a harsh taste filled his mouth. Within seconds, he abandoned the box and grabbed the trash can, retching.

What must Rufina have suffered? He sat on the floor, cradling the stout metal can, and leaned his head back against the hard stone wall. He stared at the high, arched ceilings, and wondered where she'd been imprisoned. If she'd had the ability to curse him to immortality, why couldn't she have escaped? Surely no fortress or prison could have held her.

And now that she was dead, he wondered, what did that mean for him? He spit into the can, then wiped his mouth with the back of his hand. No wonder all his years of sacrifice hadn't worked. He could sacrifice for another millennium and the curse wouldn't end, if Rufina's death meant the curse couldn't be broken.

He let out a mocking laugh. What would the professors at the University of San Rimini make of his predicament? Their offices contained floor-to-ceiling treatises on the country's history, which made the learned men perfect consultants as he'd pursued his quest for Rufina. But what would they say if he asked, "Hey, gentlemen, what's the deal with ancient San Riminian curses? Anyone know what's required to break one? It was cast by tossing this stinging green powder on the victim, you see. Any theories on that? Anyone with a position paper? Anyone want to toss me in a padded room and throw away the key? Bet I last longer than the padding!"

He set the can on the floor, then used his foot to send it careening across the smooth stone floor back to its usual spot beside the desk. Leaning his head back until it hit the wall, he closed his eyes.

An image of Isabella diTalora filled his vision. Her cute, swingy ponytail and impossibly nerdy black-rimmed glasses, the look of elation on her face over a simple dinner out, the need and desire in her expressive eyes as her fingertips wandered over his chest, the puffiness of her sweet mouth after they'd shared kisses in the bakery's back room.

He ground his fists against his eye sockets. No, he couldn't survive many more years without being able to share human emotions, without touching a woman or having her return his affections. Without being able to hold Isabella.

Tears burned his eyes, and for the first time he could remember since he was a young boy, he dropped his head onto his knees and let them come. And once they started, all eight hundred-plus years of frustration and loneliness followed.

Isabella paused at the top of the stone steps. The

storeroom door had been left open a crack, and from within, she heard what sounded like an animal cry of agony. She glanced behind her, then slowly opened the door far enough to slip inside. Softly, so as not to be seen, she descended the shadowed steps, then peeked around the doorway into the storeroom.

What she saw made her heart ache and her eyes fill with sympathetic tears. She'd seen her father cry once, the morning after her mother passed away. And she'd been privy to Federico's emotional battle after he lost Lucrezia. But never had she witnessed a man so clearly distraught as Nick Black.

He didn't see her come up beside him. When she knelt down, he jerked in surprise, but without saying a word she pulled his large body into her arms and ran her hand over his soft black hair, hoping her presence might give him a measure of peace. He quieted instantly, though his chest continued to heave and his breath came in short rasps.

"You should go, Princess. I didn't—"

"It's all right," she whispered.

"I just had some bad news is all." He raised his head off his bent knees, but didn't face her. "I haven't lost it or anything."

"You'd be the last person to 'lose it,' I suspect."

His mouth tilted up at that, and he laughed, the same odd, self-deprecating laugh she'd heard that day back in his office when she told him the job would be the opportunity of a lifetime.

"Nick, why don't you tell me what's going on? This has to do with whatever you wouldn't tell me in the bakery the other night, doesn't it?"

"It does." He turned his face to hers. The skin at

the corners of his eyes puckered in weariness, and he had bags underneath them from lack of sleep. She noticed the usual clear plastic aspirin bottle on his desk had been replaced by a green one, and wondered if his headaches were getting worse, given his apparent stress level.

"But you still feel you can't tell me."

"I wish I could, Princess, but this isn't the time to—"

"I suspect you have plenty of time." She dropped her rear down on the floor beside his, pulled the black-and-white photograph out of the pocket of her slacks, then held it in front of her, where they both could see it. "This is you, isn't it, Nick?"

He didn't answer for a moment. He simply stared at the photograph. When he spoke, his voice came out in a rasp. "Where did you get it?"

"I did some checking into your background." Before he could argue, she put a hand on his forearm. "It's not what you think. I trust you completely. But I was worried about you. I think you know me well enough by now to realize I can't resist helping anyone who's in need."

He let out a deep breath and took the photo from her. "Who found it?"

"Jack Donnington, my father's chief of security. He's the only one who has seen it, and I've sworn him to secrecy. He's British, a former MI6 man, so I think you can trust him to keep his word."

Nick's forehead creased as he pondered that. "What else did you find?"

"That you're essentially an invisible man. No birth

records—none that check out, anyway—no parents. No anything.''

''And this Mr. Donnington figured that out?''

''Yes.''

Nick flipped the picture between his fingers, his nerves clearly raw. ''I assume you have a lot of questions.''

She allowed her fingers to drift over his strong, solid forearm. Despite the short time they'd known each other, she felt comfortable in his presence, even now, when he seemed emotionally spent. ''This photo was taken in 1937, Nick. Yet you haven't aged a single day since then. Not one.''

He looked at her, his shadowed eyes confirming her words without the need to speak. ''It was the day of the Hindenburg disaster,'' he began quietly, turning his gaze back to the photo. ''I was working in a hospital near Lakehurst, volunteering my time. Then they called for ambulances, and we couldn't get to the airfield fast enough. Those poor people had such terrible burns... Do you know I can still sometimes smell the blood and burning flesh?'' He shook his head, as if he could loosen the thought from his mind. ''A press photographer captured a shot of me loading one of the victims into an ambulance. I didn't realize it until later, when the photo appeared in the paper. Your man Donnington is good. I believe this is the only photograph of me ever circulated in public. I've been very careful—''

''Nick, how old are you?''

''Ah, the important question.'' He let out a sarcastic snort. ''Thing is, you won't believe the answer, whether I tell you I'm twenty-seven or a hundred and twenty-seven, so trust me when I say you don't want to pursue this conversation." He stood up, shaking off her touch. "You'd have Mr. Donnington down here with an entire security team, ready to lock me up. In fact," he gestured to a cardboard box on his desk, "I've decided that despite the wonderful opportunity you've presented me here, I cannot stay. I'm arranging for another expert to come in and continue my work, and I'm sure—"

She stood, drawing herself up to her full height, though she still stood several inches below Nick. In the most commanding, I'm-a-princess-and-you'd-better-listen-to-me voice she could muster, she said, "No. No, you're not leaving, and no, no one will lock you up. But I want to know here and now what's going on with you."

He balked, and before she could stop herself, she reached up to cup his cheeks with her palms and caress his stubble-roughened skin. "Whatever your secret is, you can tell me. I'll believe you." At the obvious look of doubt in his eyes, she said the words she never before believed she could. "I love you, Nick. I love you with all my heart. And if I can take away your pain, I want to try."

His eyes hardened, but he didn't shake off her touch this time. "I was born in 1163, Your Highness. If you want to know how old I am, you do the math. No amount of love or understanding can take away that fact or the pain that goes with it. Wish it were so."

She took an involuntary step back and gasped. He couldn't possibly have said what she thought she heard. It wasn't possible. "Did you say 1163?"

"One, one, six, three." He cocked an eyebrow at her and hooked his thumbs through the belt loops at his hips. "You want to know why I know so much about every piece of ancient junk in this room? Why I know how to hold a sword, or how many days it took a medieval monk to transcribe a sermon or il-luminate a manuscript? It's not because I have a fancy degree. I never wrote a dissertation or even studied history, for that matter. I lived it. All of it."

Chapter Ten

Her heart wanted to believe him, just as she'd promised, but her brain wouldn't allow it. "Nick, that would make you nearly a thousand years old. That's ridiculous."

"Now tell me I'm not crazy."

She shook her head slowly, thinking over every word he'd uttered since they'd met, every action he'd taken. "No, I know you're not crazy." She glimpsed the aspirin bottle on the desk again, but forced herself to focus on him.

"Trying to convince yourself? That's understandable." He strode to the desk and picked up the bottle between his index and middle finger and swung it in front of her face. "As I told you before, I had a serious head injury. That's why I pop these things like they were candy. I was thrown from my horse in the winter of 1190, while crossing Italy. I fell down a hillside and lay in the brush for days before some local villagers found me and carried me to one of their homes for care. If it wasn't for the curse, I probably wouldn't have survived it. Anyway, needless to say, I can't exactly waltz into a doctor's office and explain my medical history. So I suffer the headaches. And that's all they are. Headaches, not delusions, though there are days I'd rather be delusional than immortal. But I don't get a choice.''

Taking the bottle from his fingers and placing it on the desktop gave her a second to think. She sank into the desk chair, trying to keep her mind open, despite the impossibility of Nick's words. ''What do you mean by 'the curse'? Are you saying you don't age—that you're *immortal*—because you're cursed?''

He nodded. ''Now you see why I don't exactly parade myself out in public, why I keep my own counsel about my past. People would categorize me as one of those whack-jobs who stand out in the desert waiting for the UFOs to arrive.''

''Tell me everything. Please.''

His gaze bored into hers, but she refused to waver, knowing he tested her with each word and each look. ''I have to know you believe me, first. Telling you this puts me at great risk, as you might imagine. It's bad enough your father's chief of security knows there's something wrong with me.''

Isabella sucked in a deep breath of the cool storeroom air. How many afternoons had she spent with mental health professionals, learning about the breadth of the problem, about the diagnosis and treatment of mental illness and about what she could do to help? Her education on the subject, balanced against the time she'd spent alone with Nick, left her confused. A mental health expert would instantly conclude he suffered from delusions, but looking at him now, she wasn't so sure.

"You believe what you're saying. So if you tell me your story, I'll believe it, too. And I promise, if you don't want me to tell anyone else, I will not." She made an *X* on her chest with her index finger. "Cross my heart and hope to die."

"Hope to die? That's not funny." He shot her a grin, but a muscle twitched in his jaw, betraying his sense of unease.

She held out her hand to him. "Have you ever told anyone?"

He stared at her outstretched fingers for a moment, then surprised her by taking her hand and kissing it. "A couple times, early on. Only my wife knew the whole story. It always turned out badly, especially in her case."

"You were married, then?" Jealousy pricked at her, but in the same instant, she realized that his wife was probably long dead. And he'd been forced to endure the loss of a spouse, just as her father and Federico had. "What was her name?"

He gave a too-casual shrug, one that only showed her more intensely the depth of his pain. "Doesn't matter."

Pulling him closer, she whispered, "I want to know anyway."

"Why?"

She tilted her chin up to him. "You were the first person who ever understood my loneliness. How I could be surrounded by people, yet live so apart. Now I know why."

Emotion flickered in his eyes, and she stood to brush his lips with a reassuring kiss. "Nick, you took away my loneliness. Let me take away yours. Or at least try."

He dropped his forehead against hers, and then for the next three hours, he talked. Hesitantly at first, but once he realized she wouldn't interrupt, and that she genuinely wanted to know his tale, with more passion. Nick hadn't believed the curse at first; he'd never put stock in tales about witches with mystical powers. But as time dragged on, and he'd still maintained his youth while those around him—including his beautiful wife—aged and died, he'd been forced to accept its truth.

As he described the witch, what happened to him in the woods and with his family, and then his years wandering through Europe, Isabella found her admiration for him growing, and the last of her doubts washing away. No one could make up a story like Nick's—at least not with the historical detail he did.

Besides, other than the unbelieveable fact that he was over eight hundred years old, everything he said clicked with something specific she'd observed about him. His reaction to seeing the keep, his knowledge of the artifacts—including the fact that the door to the storage area was the original—and even the fact he'd obviously had terrible medical care earlier in his life. As a twelfth-century knight, he'd been lucky to make it to twenty-seven, the age at which he'd been cursed, since he'd embarked on his career as a fighter at the tender age of fifteen.

What pained her the most, however, was the fact he'd given up. After centuries of battling the curse, sacrificing as no man in the history of the world, and then finally searching for answers through research, he'd admitted defeat. Right on the floor of the palace's former armory, where he'd spent so many of his earliest years. Now she understood why the cries she'd overheard were filled with such hopelessness.

"Please stay," she urged once he'd finished his tale. They were both sitting on the floor now, shoulder-to-shoulder, their backs against the stone wall. "You still might find something else here. Something that could break the curse. And if you're willing, you can visit my private physician. I've known him since I was a small child. He signed a confidentiality agreement with our family long ago, and he's never violated it. If I ask him to keep your condition to himself, he will. And he can get you the medical care you need for your headaches."

She put a hand on his knee, and met his dark, pained gaze. "I hate to see you suffer, Nick. You've suffered enough, don't you think?"

"I don't know." His voice was flat as he added, "Because of my actions, my choices, someone died. Or at least, I thought he died. Someone innocent."

"I think you've punished yourself enough for that. Far more than Rufina could have."

"Still." He swallowed audibly, then turned his head to study her. "You have no idea how tempting your offer is to me, but the risk is too great. If I stay, there's a chance the tabloids will get wind of it. Even if there's a hint that something is amiss with me—a palace employee—they'll dig and dig until they find something to pin on you. It'll be the Harvard incident magnified a thousand times."

"I don't care," she could hear her voice edging toward hysteria and tried to bring it down a notch, but couldn't. "I can't let you go, Nick. And as scared as I am of what the tabloids might say, I love you more. This past week, I realized that without you I'm not living a full life. I want you here for me, as much as I want you to stay for your own benefit."

"That's what frightens me." He was quiet for a moment before adding, "It broke my heart to watch my wife give up her friends, her social life—even her dreams of having a child—all because she thought she should stick by me until the curse was broken."

He reached over to her, running his fingers along the curve of her cheek, then tucking a stray curl behind her ear. Though his touch was gentle, the seriousness of his expression sent her heart plummeting. "I love you, too, Isabella. More than I've ever loved any woman, including my wife. I want you to live your life to the fullest, to break free of the restrictions you feel upon you to find love and happiness. But not with me. I would rather live another thousand years than see you devastated by the curse the way it devastated my wife. That's why I cannot stay."

Hot tears pricked at her eyes, as they had several times while he told his story. But this time, she couldn't prevent them from burning a path down her cheek. "Nick, you owe it to yourself to stay. It's the only chance you have to break the curse. Don't you see—"

"Sir." A voice came from the entryway behind them, causing Nick to drop his hand from Isabella's face and jump in shock. "I'd prefer to stay. Perhaps you should consider it."

Nick pushed to his feet, then offered Isabella a hand up. The princess must have left the door open behind her, or he'd have heard Anne's approach. He hadn't heard Isabella come in, but then again, he wasn't exactly listening at the time.

His heart raced, filling with fear for Isabella and her family. How much had Anne heard?

"Anne?" He raised an eyebrow in question, but his secretary's hard stare let him know that while she might not have heard everything, she'd certainly heard enough.

"I know I shouldn't have eavesdropped, sir. But I did. And I believe you should stay."

Nick glanced at Isabella. Worry lines etched her forehead, and he didn't like it.

He turned back to his secretary, who seemed strangely calm given the situation, and addressed her in as solemn a tone as he could muster. "I want you to forget what you might have heard. Or thought you heard. We are going back to Boston as soon as possible. If your fifteen years of employment with me have meant anything to you, respect my wishes on this. It has nothing to do with you. Understood?"

"I beg to differ. It has everything to do with me."

If he'd suspected the palace walls somehow intimidated Anne, or left her feeling squirrely, he'd been mistaken. She'd never spoken in such a frank, brazen manner before. As far as he could remember, she'd never even contradicted him. The short hairs on his nape prickled, but before he could open his mouth, Isabella's smooth voice interrupted.

"Anne, what do you mean?"

Anne continued to stare straight at him, her shoulders squared, her chin at a defiant angle. "If those fifteen years mean anything to you, sir, then you should take a minute to hear me out. Once you do, I believe you'll stay."

Feeling outflanked, Nick crossed his arms over his chest. "Fine. But you won't change my mind."

Anne nodded toward the princess. "You told Princess Isabella that to break the curse, you'd need to sacrifice. Right?"

"According to what Rufina said, yes."

"Until the past few weeks, you've never done that."

Nick ground his teeth to keep from saying something he shouldn't in the presence of women. Anne obviously hadn't overheard everything he'd told Isabella—at least not about the years he'd spent cleaning up muck from the floors of medieval hospitals, or about giving away every cent he had to his name, volunteering his time and labor in the most dank and disgusting places on earth. If she didn't consider that sacrifice, then what was?

Anne raised a palm in the air to stop him from arguing. "Sir, everything you've done, you've done for yourself. True, others benefitted from your work. Greatly. But you only did those things to break the curse. I know you grew to appreciate that you could help people, and at times even enjoyed doing so, but deep down you did it for yourself."

In that moment, something crumbled inside Nick. This morning, he'd come to the conclusion that he'd spent his life beating his head against the wall, trying to break the curse. But only because he thought Rufina had died. If what Anne said was true, then perhaps there was still hope.

It also meant he was as shallow and uncaring as Rufina accused him of being. A man unable to sacrifice. After so many years of thinking he had done more, sacrificed more than any man alive, the realization he'd done nothing that qualified as a sacrifice stung.

Isabella put a hand on his lower back, and again he felt humbled by her ability to sense when he needed comforting. The princess directed her attention to Anne, however. "Then what did you mean when you said 'until the past few weeks'? Has something changed?"

Anne beamed at the question. "Nick—Domenico—returned to San Rimini for the sole purpose of breaking the curse. He even risked being discovered, because he thought he had a good chance of doing so. But as he got to know you, he risked discovery for another reason."

Nick blinked. "I wanted to take Isabella out. To show her that she could experience life. That she didn't have to live the way I have." He frowned at Anne. "No, that's too simple. That's no sacrifice. I did it because I wanted to."

"You wanted it for her instead of yourself." Anne shrugged, though she continued to smile. "And it is just that simple. And now, because you fear she'll suffer the same fate as Coletta, you're willing to leave San Rimini. You're willing to give up the only chance you thought you had to break the curse, to give up a chance at love with a woman who wants to be with you and to give up a chance to be close to the royal family, which was what got you in this predicament in the first place. That's a true sacrifice. One that doesn't benefit you in any way, and in fact, can only hurt you.''

"No.'' After years of searching, this couldn't possibly be the answer. ''No. I'm leaving because I love her, not as a sacrifice—''

Nick felt Isabella's hand twitch on his back. ''Nick, was Coletta your wife's name?''

''What?''

''Coletta.'' Isabella's voice was low, strained. ''Anne mentioned the name Coletta. Yet you never did. Not tonight, not to me.''

A hard lump formed in Nick's gut. Hadn't he said Coletta's name? Surely he had. But the calculating look on Anne's face said otherwise. In that moment, everything finally made sense. His jaw dropped and his entire body tensed with the realization.

''You're Rufina, aren't you?'' he whispered. Her hair was red, though now it was streaked with gray, and she was older than the Rufina he remembered. Shorter. More calm. But then again, during their brief encounter Rufina had been beating her way through the dense brush of San Rimini's borderlands, searching for her missing son. How could he not have seen it? ''You *are* Rufina. How is that possible?''

One side of her mouth curved up. ''How is it possible that you're immortal? How is it possible that it took you eight hundred long years to figure something out that could have been done in a day?''

Her expression turned serious as she added, ''If only you'd let Coletta go, or done something that was one hundred percent for someone else, this curse would have been broken long ago.''

"All this time.'' Nick stared at Rufina, trying to absorb her words. She'd been under his nose for the past fifteen years. And probably a lot longer. He wasn't sure whether to hug her, if the curse was indeed broken, or throttle her for all the pain she'd caused him. Then he remembered.

"I'm so sorry about Ignacio. I've never forgotten him. You have no idea how many times I've wished I could tell you that. Or wished that I could make it right.''

"I know. And I know that you truly are sorry.'' Rufina withdrew an envelope from a pocket on the side of her purse, then handed it to Isabella. "He asked me to buy plane tickets back to Boston. This one's in his name. I put him in your hands now.''

The witch's face filled with a quiet warmth, and she laid her hand on Isabella's shoulder, in the same manner a grandmother might when a young child had done something particularly endearing. "You have taught him more in a month than I could in centuries of following him around the world. Perhaps,'' she flashed a quick smile at Nick, then turned back to Isabella, "perhaps you were his destiny all along.''

With that, she strode out of the room. Nick stared after her, unable to believe what just happened. He had so many questions—

Forgetting Isabella for the moment, he sprinted up the stairs, hoping to catch Rufina. But when he got to the top of the stairs, she was nowhere to be seen. He thundered down the long hallway connecting the keep with the main palace, looking into open doors as he went, until he he rounded a corner and came face-to-face with Nerina.

"What is going on here?" she demanded. "Is the princess all right?"

"I—" Nick stopped cold. "I was searching for someone. My, uh, my secretary. Did she come this way?"

Nerina frowned. "Your *secretary?* What secretary?"

He studied Nerina's face. No, she'd truly never met Anne. Either Anne—Rufina—had somehow managed to erase Nerina's knowledge of her presence, or he'd truly gone over the edge.

Entirely possible, given what had happened to him in the past few hours.

Behind him, he could hear the click-click of high heels against the sleek palace floors, approaching at a jog.

"My apologies, Nerina. I meant that I was looking for *a* secretary. I…" He improvised what he hoped was a believable excuse for tearing through the palace halls, "I just wanted to catch you before you went home for the night, to see if you could assist me."

Nerina looked past him, then gave a curt, professional bow. "Your Highness."

Nick turned to see Isabella, her face flushed from running to catch him. At least *her* presence in the storeroom hadn't been a figment of his imagination. "Princess. I was just asking Nerina about hiring a secretary."

Isabella's eyes widened.

"Your Highness?" Nerina pulled out her electronic

organizer, "did you want me to hire a secretary for Mr. Black? I wasn't aware—"

Isabella waved for her to put the organizer away. "Don't worry about it, Nerina. I'll handle it myself."

Nerina looked as if she might drop the expensive device. "Are you certain?"

"Certain. Please, spend the evening with your husband at home. If I need any assistance, I'll give you a call."

Nerina's face showed her confusion, but to her credit, she didn't question the princess. "All right. I'll be here at 6:30 a.m. We can go over your schedule then."

"Thank you, Nerina."

When the secretary was out of earshot, Isabella grabbed Nick's elbow, and without speaking, guided him first down one hall, then another. They passed a guard, who straightened at the sight of the princess, then entered what Nick immediately realized was the princess's private apartments.

"Princess—"

She spun to face him. "At this point, I really think you should call me Isabella. Don't you?"

Nick stared at her for a moment, then allowed the stress of the day to roll off him. He flopped in a delicate velvet-covered chair, belatedly hoping it could handle his weight. "I don't know what to think anymore. About anything."

Isabella fell to her knees in front of him, and grabbed his hands in hers. "Then let me do the thinking. Stay. There's no harm in it now."

"So you did see Anne."

She rolled her eyes, and he would have laughed at

the incongruity of the beautiful, polished princess making such a gesture if the situation wasn't so serious. And if he hadn't seen her do it before. "Of course I saw Anne."

"Nerina didn't. Didn't even know who I was talking about."

"I gathered that." She squeezed his hands to drive her point home. "Doesn't that tell you what you should believe? Rufina was real. And so are her powers. I can't say I understand them, but…" Isabella shrugged, then shot him a megawatt smile that would have made the paparazzi drool. "I'm willing to bet the curse truly is broken. Willing to bet my future on it, in fact. Stay. Finish the museum project. See my doctor and get your headaches cured."

"I don't know." He looked down at her lean, manicured fingers, interwoven with his scarred ones. He didn't feel any different. Not physically. If the curse had been broken, wouldn't he feel different?

"Do it for me." Isabella rose up enough to look him in the eye. "Even if you believe it's a risk to your privacy. Even if you think I'll be hurt. Just give me six months, until the museum opening. Given how long you've lived, six months is nothing. By then, we'll know if the curse is broken. If it's not, then we'll decide what to do. And if it is…"

Her amber eyes filled with tears of joy, and Nick fought to control his own response. He hardly believed it possible.

"I love you, Isabella." He pulled her into his lap, then held her tight. "I'll give you six months. And if we're lucky, I'll give you the rest of my life."

Epilogue

Nick's arm tightened around Isabella's waist as they circled the dance floor in the museum's grand marble atrium. The light of the full moon streamed in through the glass ceiling, five floors above their heads. All around them, on the four stories of balconies surrounding the atrium, couples chatted, drank champagne and discussed the artifacts they'd seen during their tour of the museum's new wing, now officially open and dedicated to Isabella's mother, the late Queen Aletta.

"It's magical, isn't it?" Isabella murmured in his ear.

"Magic. That's one way to describe tonight." Nick grinned as they spun to the gentle strains of the San Rimini Royal Orchestra, set up on the opposite side of the atrium. "But yes, it truly is. You've pulled it off. And from the look on your father's face tonight, you've made him a very happy man."

"I think so." She smiled. Her features seemed lit from within as they spun between two other couples, then passed by Crown Prince Antony and his wife, Princess Jennifer. "And you seem to be a very happy man, too."

"How did you guess?" He laughed. "You know, Jack Donnington is an impressive man. Without his help, I wouldn't be here tonight." Over the past six months, Donnington had used his skills to fill in the gaps in Nick's history. If a tabloid reporter went scrounging into Nick's past, they'd find he had an unquestionable background. And one entirely suited to a man about to propose marriage to San Rimini's only princess.

Isabella looked up at Nick and smiled, which prompted a flurry of activity amongst the photographers lining the atrium walls, all of whom jockeyed for position to capture the first-ever photos of the princess kissing a man.

"You know," she teased, "without all *you've* done, none of us would be here tonight." She reached up to run her fingers through his hair, then stopped short.

"Follow me."

Nick frowned at Isabella's sudden seriousness, but allowed her to guide him away from the dance floor, toward one of the museum's hallways.

"Arturo and Paolo aren't expecting us tonight, Isabella."

"I know," she replied, "though I'm terribly jealous that they prefer to hear their stories from you now."

"Hey, I can't help it if I've got more stories to tell.

Maybe tomorrow night I'll tell them about Napoleon and Josephine.''

"Don't you dare!''

He smiled to himself, then asked, "So where are you taking me?''

"Here.'' She stopped in front of an oversized gilt mirror, then turned him to face it.

"What?''

"Notice anything?''

He stared at himself, seeing the same reflection he'd seen for nearly a thousand years. "No.''

Then he noticed it. Just at his temple, a gray hair stood out amidst the black.

"That's the story you should tell Arturo and Paolo,'' she said, her rich voice cracking as she spoke. "The fairy tale of *The Cursed Knight*. Because now it has a happy ending.''

*   *   *   *   *

DEBBIE

NEW YORK TIMES BESTSELLING AUTHOR

MACOMBER

*illuminates women's lives
with compassion, with love
and with grace. In Changing Habits
she proves once again why she's
one of the world's most popular writers
of fiction for—and about—women.*

Changing Habits

*Available the first week of May 2003
wherever hardcovers are sold!*

MIRA®

Don't miss the latest miniseries from award-winning author Marie Ferrarella:

Meet...

Sherry Campbell—ambitious newswoman who makes headlines when a handsome billionaire arrives to sweep her off her feet...and shepherd her new son into the world!
A BILLIONAIRE AND A BABY, SE#1528, available March 2003

Joanna Prescott—Nine months after her visit to the sperm bank, her old love rescues her from a burning house—then delivers her baby....
A BACHELOR AND A BABY, SD#1503, available April 2003

Chris "C.J." Jones—FBI agent, expectant mother and always on the case. When the baby comes, will her irresistible partner be by her side?
THE BABY MISSION, IM#1220, available May 2003

Lori O'Neill—A forbidden attraction blows down this pregnant Lamaze teacher's tough-woman facade and makes her consider the love of a lifetime!
BEAUTY AND THE BABY, SR#1668, available June 2003

The Mom Squad—these single mothers-to-be are ready for labor...and true love!

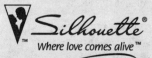

SILHOUETTE *Romance*®

COMING NEXT MONTH

#1666 PREGNANT BY THE BOSS!—Carol Grace
Champagne under the mistletoe had led to more than kisses for
tycoon Joe Callaway and his assistant. Unwilling to settle for less
than true love, Claudia Madison left him on reluctant feet. Could
Joe win Claudia back in time to hear the pitter-patter of new ones?

#1667 BETROTHED TO THE PRINCE—Raye Morgan
Catching the Crown
Sometimes the beautiful princess needed to dump her
never-met betrothed—at least that's what independent
Tianna Roseanova-Krimorova thought. But a mystery baby,
a mistaken identity and a surprisingly sexy prince soon made
her wonder if fairy-tale endings weren't so bad after all!

#1668 BEAUTY AND THE BABY—Marie Ferrarella
The Mom Squad
Widowed, broke and pregnant, Lori O'Neill longed for a knight.
And along came…*her brother-in-law?* Carson O'Neill had always
done the right thing. But the sweet seductress made this Mr. Nice
Guy think about being very, very naughty!

#1669 A GIFT FROM THE PAST—Carla Cassidy
Soulmates
Could Joshua McCane and his estranged wife ever agree on anything? But Claire needed his help, so he reluctantly offered his
services. Soon, their desire for each other threatened to rage out of
control. Was Joshua so sure their love was gone?

#1670 TUTORING TUCKER—Debrah Morris
The headline: "West Texas Oil Field Foreman Brandon Tucker
Wins $50 Million, Hires Saucy, Sexy Trust Fund Socialite
To Teach Him The Finer Things In Life." The *Finer Things*
course study: candlelight kisses, slow, sensual waltzes, velvety
soft caresses…

#1671 OOPS…WE'RE MARRIED?—SUSAN LUTE
When career-driven Eleanor Rose wanted to help charity, she
wrote a check. She did *not* marry a man who wanted a mother
for his son and a comfortable wife for himself. She did *not*
become Suzy Homemaker…*nor* give in to seductive glances…
or passionate kisses…or fall in love. Or did she?

SRCNM0503